Resa

Harlequin
Romance

OTHER
Harlequin Romances
by ELIZABETH ASHTON

THE ROCKS
OF ARACHENZA

by

ELIZABETH ASHTON

HARLEQUIN BOOKS   TORONTO
WINNIPEG

Original hard cover edition published in 1973
by Mills & Boon Limited.

© Elizabeth Ashton 1973

SBN 373-01810-X

Harlequin edition published September 1974

Printed in Canada

CHAPTER ONE

THE golden Italian sunlight poured down into the little courtyard at the back of the hotel, which was overlooked by a medley of wrought iron balconies. Wisteria, with its clusters of papery mauve flowers, draped one wall; a tub full of scarlet geraniums occupied a corner; a mangy cat was performing its ablutions in its centre, enjoying the warm spring sunshine.

A girl with a mop of black hair crept out of the kitchen quarters, looking cautiously about her to make sure that she was alone. She had counted upon the hotel visitors either being out, or having a siesta. Believing herself to be unobserved, she ran to open a door in the outer wall to admit a bronzed youth.

The next moment they were locked in each other's arms, and at that precise instant, Lorena Lawrence came out on to her own little balcony on the third floor and looked down at the entwined figures. She recognised the girl, Maria, who was employed in this small hotel, where she was staying during her visit to Rome. Very fair herself, she had admired her olive skin and big dark eyes. It was obvious that Maria had taken advantage of the siesta hour to meet her lover, and it was equally obvious from their behaviour that they were very much in love.

To be in love was a state of being which Lorena had not yet experienced, and she did not think that she ever would. The indulged daughter of a prosperous Lincolnshire farmer, she had been too busy with her tennis and riding to spare much time for romantic yearnings. She had during her teens suffered the usual schoolgirl crushes for unattainable idols, usually pop singers, but she had outgrown those juvenile fancies. The brash young farmers and similar types which she had met at the hunt balls and other social functions had been good playmates, but none of them had touched her emotions. Then she had decided upon modelling as her career, a profession which was remote from the life to which she had been reared, but which had attracted her by its dissimilarity. To her surprise and that of her parents, she had met with almost instantaneous success, and from that point onwards her career had absorbed her to the exclusion of anything else. She dimly surmised that at some distant date, when modelling began to pall, she would take up with some steady young man and settle down to domesticity, but as for the raptures and agonies of being in love, she did not believe she was capable of experiencing them. Passion had never stirred her; she regarded it as a mysterious, rather puzzling force. She had had her share of masculine admiration, but for the most part she had found it could be very inconvenient, leading as it so often did to awkward situations. Occasionally she had flirted when a good-looking man had caught her fancy, but she had always drawn back when he became amorous, and she looked with slight scorn upon her friends' emotional tangles, which always seemed to her to be so foolish. No woman need become involved to the point of desperation, she insisted, and she could not conceive of being herself involved in such a predicament. She was devoutly thankful that she was by nature cool and sensible, not realising that up to the present, although she was twenty-two years old, she was still completely unawakened.

She contemplated the tableau below her depicting love's young dream, half curiously, half contemptuously. Maria would earn a rating, possibly even be dismissed if she were caught. Yet she was ready to risk her job for a kiss. An expensive indulgence, Lorena though wryly, and wondered if she herself was missing something, but if she were, she was sure it was an experience she was better without.

The door behind her slammed as someone impetuously

entered her bedroom, and she left the balcony and the drama in the courtyard to encounter her visitor.

The tall red-haired girl who had burst into her privacy so unceremoniously was Venetia Manners, a mannequin employed by the same couture house which had engaged Lorena as a replacement for its top model who had fallen ill upon the eve of showing the collection. The House had been delighted when their agency ascertained that 'Lorena' (already she had made her name) was free, and as she always enjoyed foreign assignments, she had accepted with alacrity.

The Manners family, although of British birth, lived in Italy, and Venetia had been pleased to welcome a compatriot. Together they had supported each other throughout the frenzied weeks of completing and showing the collection, and had become firm friends. Now Venetia was due for a holiday, and Lorena was going home.

Her sudden appearance this afternoon astonished Lorena, who understood she meant to rest all day.

'This is a surprise!' she exclaimed, thinking how very striking Venetia was, with her gorgeous red hair and large brown eyes. 'I thought you'd be flat out after all your labours. I know I've been feeling as limp as a jellyfish.'

'I've something here that'll put new life into you,' Venetia declared, waving a piece of paper. 'A note from Signora Ricci.'

'That friend of your mother's who came to see the collection?' Lorena enquired.

'Right first time, and guess what—she's sent a formal invitation asking me and a friend to spend a week at their villa on the Costa Smeralda. A whole week by the sea, Rena, with an exciting house party and a private plane laid on to get us there. That's the sort of money the Riccis have got, and we'll be lapped in luxury all the way. You'll come, won't you?'

'It's very kind of you to ask me,' Lorena said a little

doubtfully, for the prospect of a smart house party composed of strangers was a little daunting, 'but I'm expected at home.'

'Tell your people you've been delayed,' Venetia commanded. 'You don't have to go, do you? No immediate engagements? You said you too were going to have a rest. Sardinia will be much more relaxing than England where the reports say the weather is anything but springlike.'

That was confirmed by Lorena's last letter from her mother, in which she complained that they were enduring a cold, grey May, as that month sometimes was.

She looked at the brilliant sunshine outside the window. She had thought that it was a shame to be leaving Italy at its loveliest to return to the bleak Northland, and the Costa Smeralda she knew was one of the most beautiful coasts on the Mediterranean.

'If it's only for a week . . .' she began hesitatingly.

'Unfortunately, yes, but it'll be a week to remember. Oh, Rena, just think of it, miles of silver sand and a green-blue sea under an azure sky with bathing and boating every day. Can you resist it?'

'Sounds glorious,' Lorena agreed. She was tempted to accept, but Venetia's next words gave her pause.

'I think asking us was Signor Ricci's idea, not his wife's. He came with her the day we were showing the beach wear and thought we'd be a decorative addition to his house party. He's probably short of girls to amuse his business buddies who leave their wives at home when they go on the spree. He asked me if we could dance, swim and play tennis, all of which you do adequately, so you'll be paying for your keep, so to speak.' Her eyes narrowed with a calculating look in them. 'His pals are all loaded, and we might pick up rich husbands.'

'But I don't want a husband,' Lorena objected.

'You should look ahead. Mannequins don't last for ever, and we should cash in upon our assets while we've got

8

them.' She sat down, in a wicker chair, stretching her long legs. 'I mean to. Papa's got nothing to leave me, and I like luxury. If I don't get it, I shall become a remarkably catty old spinster.'

'You don't need to be that,' Lorena said, laughing. 'I'm sure you've had heaps of proposals.'

Venetia looked mournful. 'They all seemed to be poverty-stricken,' she complained, 'and I'm expensive. Love in a cottage doesn't appeal to me. This millionaire's paradise might produce someone who'd fit the bill.'

'I hope it does, for your sake, but I don't think it's much in my line,' Lorena demurred.

'Then go for the ozone,' Venetia laughed. 'We'll tell any prospective suitors you're booked for a nunnery.' She plunged into a rapturous description of the island which she had once visited, and Lorena's interest was aroused. Though only about a hundred and fifty miles long, Sardinia presented a great variety of scenery, and if Lorena tired of the coast, she could explore the mountains.

Lorena realised that she might never have another chance to visit this fascinating place, and felt she would be a fool if she did not take the opportunity. But she was still a little doubtful about the company, and when Venetia paused for breath she said tentatively:

'I only hope this house party isn't too permissive.'

Venetia laughed heartily.

'Oh, darling, be your age! You're no longer wet behind the ears. Surely you've learned how to cope with passes? But Signora Ricci herself is most respectable. You can walk in her shadow if you feel you need a chaperon. She's never been able to understand how Mother could let me be a model girl, Italian mamas don't think it's respectable, but she's decided it must be different for the English. There's no reason at all for you to be stuffy.'

'I'm not stuffy, but I like to know what's expected of me,' Lorena told her with a faint smile. Very fair herself,

9

she had suffered from the unwelcome attentions of Latin men who found her delicate blonde colouring irresistible, and she was suspicious of the frivolous sort of people of whom Signor Ricci's house party would doubtless consist.

'All that will be expected of you is to have a good time,' Venetia said emphatically.

Lorena looked again out of the window at the glowing sunlight. Cloud-bound England was not attractive, and after all it would only be for a week.

'If you'd really rather have me than anybody else, I'd love to come,' she told Venetia. 'It's very nice of you to want me.'

Venetia said:

'Of course I want you. You're not a cat and you always play fair, which is more than can be said for most of the girls I know.' She sprang up from her seat and seizing Lorena round the waist, waltzed her round the room. 'Whoopee, Rena, we're going to have a whale of a time!'

Lorena hoped that she was right.

When the two girls arrived at the airport, Venetia met an acquaintance at the reception desk, Marie-Céleste Duprez, a French girl who it transpired had also been invited to join the house party. She was dark and vivacious, wearing a smart silk dress and jacket with a picture hat. She eyed the other two girls a little sourly, feeling eclipsed. Tall Venetia, with her red hair, looking exotic in an emerald green swinging cloak, would be noticeable anywhere, but it was Lorena who she suspected would be a greater rival for masculine favours.

Dressed in a blue trouser suit of thin material, which set off her pale skin, which had been carefully guarded against the Italian sun, her hair was silver-gilt, her grey eyes large and candid. In spite of her recent exhausting activities, there was a dewy freshness about her, an air of youth, which made older girls look wilted. Yet there was nothing unso-

10

phisticated about her, she wore her clothes well, and knew how to make up; it was simply that she looked virginal. Marie-Céleste was well aware how such Nordic fairness would cause a furore among dark Latin men. She hoped that with such colouring Lorena might be cold and un-responsive, nullifying her appeal.

Two young men came into reception, where they were waiting. One, an Italian, wore a semi-uniform and smiled broadly, showing white teeth when he saw them.

'The *signorinas* for Signor Ricci's party?' he enquired. '*Va bene*, I am Benito, your pilot. Please go through into the departure lounge while I deal with your cases. Signor Marescu, perhaps you will escort the Signor's guests?'

The other man did not smile. He was taller than his companion with a dark, almost saturnine countenance, carry-ing himself proudly. His intensely dark eyes slid over the three girls contemptuously, but he bowed politely to them and shepherded them towards passport control. The plane was a small jet and in addition to the three girls there were a couple of middle-aged men. They chose rear seats and became engrossed in some important business conversation, with occasional sly glances towards the women. The five of them were the only passengers, though the machine could have accommodated many more. It was furnished with comfortable double seats, all facing forward, with a raised table flap in front of each. There was a stewardess, an Italian girl, in attendance in a natty uniform. Signor Mar-escu was not with them; he had joined the pilot on the flight deck.

Marie-Céleste and Venetia sat together being immersed in Roman gossip. Lorena chose a seat a little apart from them on the other side of the aisle. She did not want to listen to their chatter, which was all about people whom she did not know. She was feeling pleasantly relaxed and had no wish to talk. Their holiday had started auspiciously, and she hoped it would continue to do so.

As soon as they were airborne, the stewardess brought them a choice of refreshments, coffee, wine, cakes and fruit.

Venetia sighed contentedly. 'This is what I call travel de luxe. It augurs well for the rest of our visit.'

'But who is the satanic *monsieur*?' Marie-Célèste asked, without troubling to lower her voice. She spoke English with only a trace of accent. 'Do you suppose he is one of the guests? Me, I find him *effroyable*.'

'Just my type,' Venetia announced. 'I like a man who presents a challenge.'

'But did you not see the way in which he regarded us?' Marie-Célèste's voice was plaintive. 'As if we were something the cat had left upon the mat?'

Venetia giggled. 'I bet I can make him look at me a little more appreciatively. I'd put up with a great deal worse than that, provided he was well oiled.'

'I am sure you would, *signorina*.'

They all three started violently. Venetia and Marie-Célèste having been absorbed in their chatter, while Lorena was half asleep, they had not noticed Signor Marescu come in from the pilot's cabin. No whit discomposed, Venetia looked at him coquettishly, but he turned away from her to speak to the stewardess and Lorena heard him mutter:

'Mercenary go-getters!'

'*Si, signor*,' the stewardess said, using her fine eyes provocatively.

He was retracing his steps, when the plane gave a sudden lurch and he was flung against Lorena. She drew back, while she eyed him with cold hostility. Who was he to condemn her companions and herself so scornfully because he had overheard a joking remark of Venetia's? But he had looked at them contemptuously in reception, suspecting they were good-time girls, but why should they not have a break after working hard?

'*Scusi*,' he said, staring sombrely down into the wide grey eyes raised to his. 'It was an air pocket.'

A faint puzzlement gathered about his brow and his eyes became more intent. To her surprise he sat down beside her.

'You do not look like the others,' he told her in a low voice. His English was accentless.

'Don't I?' she returned casually. 'I am, you know, we're all fashion models'—she did not know Marie-Céleste's calling, but suspected she belonged to the sisterhood—'a mode of life which no doubt you despise, but for all that we're respectable hard-working girls, most of us.'

His fine mouth twisted satirically. 'You surprise me. I thought it was a life of ease and glamour, not to say artifice.'

Lorena was aware that her companions were throwing her amused glances, but she did not think they could overhear their conversation.

'The glamour is much overrated,' she told him. 'There's nothing glamorous about being photographed in a bikini on a beach with a north wind blowing.'

His eyes raked her as if he were stripping her in his mind, and she wished that she had not mentioned a bikini.

'It must be a delightful picture,' he said gravely. 'Your creamy skin, that silver-gilt hair—surely you come from Scandinavia? Only in the far north does one find such pale fire.'

'I'm English,' she said shortly. 'I live in England, so do my people. You, I suppose, are Italian?'

He lifted his head arrogantly.

'I am a Sard. I was born in the mountain region where life is simple and hard, but the inhabitants are genuine right through.'

'You speak English very well,' she observed, wondering if he were a sample of Signor Ricci's guests. He did not look the playboy type.

'I have been educated,' he said stiffly. 'Though I have been brought up rough, I am not a barbarian.'

13

'I'm sure you're not,' she assured him, insincerely, for he looked as if he could be definitely barbaric. 'But if you despise the *dolce vita*, how comes it you're staying with Signor Ricci?'

'I am not. Benito is giving me a lift to Olbia, that is all. I prefer to avoid the *consorcio*.'

'The what?'

'The company who are developing the land around Arachenza, the thirty-five miles of coast designated the Costa Smeralda, which Signor Ricci and ...' he hesitated, looking oddly embarrassed—'others have added to the playgrounds of Europe. I know we are all told the tourist trade is beneficial, the north-east coast was once barren and now has become a money-spinner, but prosperity and visitors are bringing in many less desirable things, so that perhaps it is a pity it was not left as it was.'

'What sort of things?' she enquired.

'A general lowering of standards, dishonesty, permissiveness and crime.'

'That sounds terrible; so you would prefer your people to remain in primitive poverty?'

'Not necessarily, but I would like them to keep their pride.'

Pride was in his own face, the fine aquiline features, the scornful mouth, the way he carried his head.

'I should have thought prosperity brought more blessings than evil,' Lorena said thoughtfully.

'And you are one of the blessings?'

The way he said it was an insult and Lorena was stung.

'*Signor*, what exactly do you think I am?' she demanded.

He smiled, a brilliant smile, which lit up his whole face, giving vividness to the intense blackness of his eyes. In repose his expression was grave and sombre, but that brief flashing smile gave a glimpse of the ardent nature beneath his habitual restraint.

'A creature of ice and snow ... and cold calculation,' he

14

told her.

'You are very sweeping in your judgments, *signor*.'

'I have met Ricci's house guests before,' he returned. 'Dewy-eyed innocence is not one of their characteristics.' He looked at her searchingly. 'Though you ape it very well.'

'I do, don't I?' she told him gaily. 'It's one of my chief assets. All the same, I don't think you should condemn me without evidence because of the company I keep.'

'It is a good way to assess a man—or a woman.'

She said nothing to that. She had not chosen her associates, she was only coming to the Costa Smeralda, as Venetia put it, for the ozone. She turned her shoulder towards her companion and stared out of the window. The aeroplane was travelling through brilliant blue sky, while beneath it a feather bed of cloud obscured the sea, but she was aware that his direct gaze was still fixed upon her, weighing her up and coming to a wrong conclusion. She decided that it was too difficult to try to correct his misconceptions, nor was it worth while since he was not a fellow guest and they were unlikely to meet again.

He said abruptly:

'You look very young and far too pretty to be travelling without a man's protection.'

A typically Latin point of view, she thought.

'That's not essential, you know,' she said demurely. 'I've toured most of the continent in the course of my job and I'm well able to take care of myself.'

'Indeed?' he sounded sceptical. 'You look so ... fragile.' His glance slid over her, noting the fineness of her bone structure, the delicacy of her features, her slim waist. 'So slender, I could break you between my two hands,' he murmured with a sort of wonder.

He was, though she did not realise it then, comparing her with his own countrywomen, who belonged to a short stocky race.

'Appearances are deceptive and I'm really very tough,' she told him, her eyes instinctively going to his hands which were folded upon his knees. They were sinewy, long-fingered hands, nicely shaped and burnt dark brown by the sun, hands which for all their slenderness would have a steely grip. In imagination she could feel them about her middle, squeezing her flesh in an attempt to span her waist, which he probably could do, since she was so slight.

She drew a deep breath and hoped she had not blushed, as she impatiently dismissed the wanton thought. She was not normally given to such flights of fancy with regard to men. What was there about this dark Sard that incited them? His masculinity, the hint of repressed violence, of passion held in leash?

Rubbish, she thought scornfully. I've met many similar types, and they didn't improve upon closer acquaintance-ship, and I'm glad I shan't meet this one again. I don't want any complications during this trip.

Yielding to a mischievous impulse, she decided that since he had so arbitrarily misjudged her, she would play along with him, and that would douse any sentimental feelings he might be harbouring in her direction. Smiling provoca-tively, she said airily:

'Girls like me, with no prospects, have to make the most of their ... assets,' she recalled Venetia's words. 'Signor Ricci's invitation presented a wonderful opportunity. I understand he has collected a herd of playboys for us to milk, a chance that doesn't often come my way.' She stole a glance at him and saw an expression of intense distaste cross his face. Gleefully, she went on:

'I might even manage to catch a rich husband if I play my cards well.'

Distaste was succeeded by the same puzzled look with which he had first encountered her. Then his face became a bland mask.

He leaned back in his seat, studying her appraisingly

through half shut eyes; his lashes she noted were very long and thick.

'Most of the Ricci clientele have already been appropriated,' he said with a drawl. 'But there is the odd bachelor or two. There's a fellow called Giulio—no one ever remembers his surname—who haunts the place, and he has a penchant for blondes. He might be worth your ammunition, but play hard to get. Not that I can teach you anything, I am sure. Incidentally, how much would you settle for?'

'Nothing less than ten thousand a year,' she flashed.

His glance slid over the thin suit she wore, which had been a reduced model.

'*Si*, you look expensive, but Giulio could afford you.'

Throughout the conversation he had been subtly insulting, and she wondered why he stayed beside her. She seemed to intrigue him in spite of his scorn, and there was a curious undercurrent to his speech about this Giulio, almost as if he were jealous of the fellow he was recommending to her. Possibly he envied the other man's wealth, and all it could buy for him.

'You say you're a Sard,' she said, anxious to change the subject. 'Are you typical of your country?'

'Not entirely,' he looked a little bleak. 'I am taller than most Sards, who are a small race, but mine is one of the oldest families on the island.'

'How nice for you! You're married, of course?'

'No, *signorina*, not yet,' his eyes became mocking. 'But I fear my income falls below your standards, and I would only marry a Sardo girl.'

'One who is from the mountains and genuine right through?' she quoted his own words back to him. 'I wonder you condescend to talk to me at all, and now you've ascertained that I'm a mercenary go-getter—your expression, *signor*—you must be glad that we shall not meet again.'

'It is a small island,' he pointed out with a flash of white

17

teeth, 'and it would be ungallant to endorse your supposition, though as I have no use for Ricci and his house parties, possibly you will prove correct.' He sounded almost regretful. 'Actually I have enjoyed our meeting. You are something of a challenge, *signorina*.'

'How intriguing!' she retorted, thinking that he presented one even more so. Suddenly she very much wanted to put herself right with him, to explain that she had been joking and in reality she had only come to see the country and give Venetia the benefit of her company, but before she could think of an opening remark, he abruptly stood up.

'I will only say *arrivederci, signorina*, and hope fate will be kind,' he told her, giving her a keen, direct look. Then, almost as if the words were forced out of him, he added:

'That hair of yours, is it natural?'

A stray sunbeam from some glass fitting in the roof had fallen upon her head, making her hair a nimbus round her face.

Surprised, she answered coldly: 'Entirely. I have never even had it tinted.'

'A gift from heaven,' he murmured. Recollecting his manners, he gave her his fascinating smile. 'Forgive me, I did not mean to be rude. It is very beautiful.'

He bowed in his foreign manner, and went to rejoin Benito.

Venetia came across to her, dropping into the seat which he had vacated.

'Well, I never!' she exclaimed. 'What was all that about? Was he telling you the story of his life?' She stared at her friend. 'It's that hair that does it. I think I'll have mine dyed.'

'I do not think that colour, or lack of colour, would suit you,' Marie-Céleste called to her, having caught the remark, for Venetia had not lowered her voice. She added cattily: 'I think it is insipid.'

The two Italians looked round curiously, and dropping

18

her voice, Venetia told Lorena:

'Of course Italians are always fascinated by pale blondes.'

'He isn't an Italian, he's a Sard,' Lorena corrected her.

'It's the same thing, isn't it?' Venetia asked carelessly.

Lorena did not think it was, but she said nothing.

The International Consortium which controlled the Costa Smeralda was still in the process of developing it. The place possessed some half a dozen hotels, while villas and shops were mushrooming over what had once been a barren area of marsh and salt pans. Roads had been built and a yacht basin constructed; it was estimated that it would take in all thirty million pounds of capital before it reached its full development. Nature had endowed it with miles of white sand beside a green-blue sea and the climate for most of the year was mild and sunny.

Signor Ricci's summer residence was more like a palace than a villa. Built entirely of white stone, its long façade was decorated with wide low arches opening on to a paved terrace overlooking the beach. Constructed in the form of a square, it enclosed an indoor swimming pool, surrounded by potted plants, in which a fountain played under a glass dome. There was an immense lounge with doors opening both on to the terrace and the patio edging the pool, which could be cleared—and was—for dancing in the evenings. At one end of it was a bar with a lavish display of every sort of drink.

The furniture in all the rooms was of light cane, for it was a place for holidays, and the floors were tiled, but there was a profusion of cushions and draperies, which gave it an air of opulence, and the wide divan beds in the guest rooms were luxurious.

Signor Ricci was a shipping magnate and he was well know in all the international resorts, the yacht clubs and the race courses. His friends were others of the same type—

continental playboys, though rather elderly boys in most cases.

Signora Ricci received her guests in the lounge when they assembled for lunch, after having been shown to their rooms by obsequious servants. She was a handsome woman, but running to fat, and exuded good nature. She greeted the three girls kindly, saying she hoped they would enjoy themselves, and told Venetia she was growing very like her mother, a remark which did not please the mannequin, who considered her mother lacked style.

Her husband welcomed them with flowery compliments —such beauty and elegance would enhance any gathering, but Lorena did not like the glint in his round dark eyes as he appraised them.

The dozen or so guests included Marie-Céleste and the two business men who had travelled on the plane, and others of a similar type. There was a sprinkling of youngsters of both sexes, but women would have been in the minority without the three models, who were the most decorative females present.

Watching them surreptitiously, while she ate the excellent luncheon served to them at small tables on the terrace, Lorena suspected that they were more than ordinarily permissive and that she would need to be on her guard. She and Venetia shared a table with a silk manufacturer from Milan, who had supplied the material for many of the gowns which they had modelled, as he hastened to inform them, and a man called Giulio whom she identified as the person her companion on the plane had mentioned. She found him repulsive. He was wiry and short with flat-lidded eyes which made her think of a reptile in a brown dissipated face. He did not talk much, but he eyed her lasciviously throughout the meal, and she had the uneasy foreboding that he was going to be a problem.

Lunch was followed by an hour's siesta and then water sports. Rocks raised grey heads along the fretted coastline, dazzling white sand stretched far out into the sea. Giulio had a motor boat and towed the more adventurous on water-skis. Lorena was content to bathe in water so clear that she could see the sand ridges and shells on the sea's floor, and wash away all the heat and dust of Rome.

Dinner was more formal, being served on one long table indoors. During the meal one of their Italian fellow-travellers mentioned that Signor Marescu had been on the aeroplane, and the Signora exclaimed:

'Why did not you ask him to join us?'

Her husband laughed. 'You know that Mario will not come here. He scorns us for a lot of lazy layabouts. He is only interested in improving the lot of his countrymen.'

'*Ecco*, surely we are all doing that?' someone interjected, and someone else added:

'He had better start with his own family. His grandmother lives in a near-hovel, I am told—his cousin is a headstrong piece who, I do not doubt, will end up in trouble, while as for his brother—if ever there was a candidate for the *banditti*, that one is.'

'Enough!' Signora Ricci said sharply. 'You are repeating ill-natured gossip, Luigi. The Marescus are a most respected family, and I for one would be honoured to have Mario at my table.'

'You will not get him,' Giulio told her with a sneer. 'He would be afraid that the gorgeous houris you have imported from the *continente*'—for so Italy was designated in Sardinia—'would tempt him from his allegiance to that black-browed gypsy to whom he is contracted. I am all for blonde women myself,' and he ogled Lorena.

The talk, which soon passed to other subjects, had recalled the Sard to Lorena. So he was called Mario Marescu, and he was, as they had said of a very different stamp from the company present. They criticised him for being a do-gooder, but none of them, she thought disparagingly, had ever done a hand's turn for anybody except themselves.

There was dancing in the evening, and Giulio insisted upon partnering her, but he was not a good dancer and she suspected that he only asked her so as to have an opportunity to touch her. She concealed her aversion with difficulty. She could not be rude to a fellow guest, but she suspected the time was not far distant when she would have to administer a definite snub.

Next day she was inveigled into a game of tennis, which was played early in the morning, before the sun grew too hot. Lorena had in her girlhood ridden and played most games, until she took up modelling and curtailed such activities for fear of becoming too muscular. She had not forgotten her old skill and acquitted herself well. Giulio partnered her opponent and was no mean player, so that she was elated when he was beaten.

As she went towards the villa to change he attached himself to her, and was loud in praise of her performance.

'The victory was due to your expertise,' he told her. 'Together we would be invincible. You must play with me at the tournament which will be held at the end of the week.'

'I understood we drew for partners,' she said stiffly, hoping chance would prevent such an eventuality.

He smiled slyly. 'These things can be arranged.'

Her attention was diverted by the sight of the two men standing on the terrace watching their approach. One was Signor Ricci, the other her acquaintance of the plane.

Giulio whistled. 'Hello, what brings the worthy Signor Marescu to our low dive? I thought he scorned our frivolities.'

Mario was wearing white flannels with a white sweater, which showed off his brown skin and inky hair. He looked tall and debonair beside Signor Ricci's embonpoint. His eyes were fixed upon Lorena and she was glad that she was wearing a dress of Wimbledon pattern and not the universal shorts. Her hair had been loosened by her exertions and hung in a tangled mass on her shoulders. She put up a hand self-consciously in a vain effort to tidy it.

Signor Ricci was chuckling as he introduced them.

22

'Signor Marescu must have heard of the lovelies we have imported from Rome and has come to look them over,' he suggested.

'My call upon you was of a business nature,' Mario said coldly. 'And I travelled with your lady guests on the same plane.'

'So you stole a march on us, eh?' Giulio sounded aggressive. 'But this one, the pick of the bunch, is my partner for the duration.'

Mario's eyes became derisive.

'I see the Signorina Lawrence has not wasted any time,' he drawled.

The blood rose in Lorena's cheeks at his tone and she said quickly: 'I refuse to tie myself to anyone. Your tennis may be good, Giulio, but your dancing isn't up to my standard.' Which was hardly polite, but he had angered her by his bland declaration of ownership.

He gave her a vindictive look, while Mario said silkily:

'I am sure you excel in all the arts, *signorina*, including that of coquetry.' The black eyes met her grey ones with a hint of challenge. 'I shall have to come one evening and test your abilities.'

'You are always welcome here,' Signor Ricci told him eagerly. 'My wife has a warm regard for you.'

'And you do not mind being the complacent husband?' Giulio asked spitefully.

'I am a tolerant man,' Signor Ricci returned. 'Which you are not, Giulio; moreover, I know I can trust Marescu.'

Giulio's expression became a sneer, but ignoring him, Signor Ricci linked his arm through Mario's.

'Come and pay your respects to the Signora, my boy, and perhaps she can persuade you to come to dinner. These two are longing for a tête-à-tête.'

Lorena felt a surge of indignation at this ill-judged remark, while Giulio looked complacent. She dared not look at Mario, who was still watching her, in fact he had kept his eyes upon her throughout the brief encounter. As he was led away, he turned his head to give her a last, lingering look. Giulio noticed it and resented it.

'What brought him here?' he grumbled. 'He usually gives us all a wide berth. Ricci is a fool to trust him; that one is a devious character.' He looked thoughtfully at Lorena. 'So you travelled out with him, did you?'

'We were on the same plane,' Lorena said stiffly.

'Don't let his romantic good looks engender any tender thoughts,' he said warningly. 'The Sards are very insular, and he is proud to be one. Rather unpleasant people, I have always found them; quick to take offence and really dangerous if they believe they are insulted. That is because they are a subject race——' he was ignoring the fact that though often invaded the Sards had never really submitted to a conqueror. 'He would never allow himself to become involved with a foreigner, however beautiful.'

'Thanks for the hint, but I've no intention of becoming involved with him or anyone else.' Lorena emphasised the last two words.

The reptilian eyes glittered. '*Chi lo sa,*' he muttered.

'Now I must have a shower,' Lorena told him firmly, and made her escape to her room.

She wondered which embarrassed her more, Mario or Giulio. Giulio she believed she could cope with, but regarding the former, she hoped he would not accept the dinner invitation and she would not see him again. There was something definitely disturbing about his keen direct gaze. She knew that he despised her, and she sensed that he was fiercely resentful of the fact that she attracted him, and he was trying to find fresh flaws in her to counter her lure. His attitude was hardly complimentary, for though he might be drawn to her outer covering he had only contempt for the creature who lived inside it, and her pride was deeply injured. She resolved not to give him another thought, and promptly thought of him all the more.

CHAPTER TWO

LORENA stood under the shower in the pink-tiled private bathroom connected with her room, and the surrounding mirrors showed endless replicas of her ivory body, like Leighton's picture of Psyche, poised upon the edge of her pool. For as yet the sun had not yet touched her, she had to be very careful not to expose her pale skin too long or too frequently to its rays, or, in spite of the use of oils and unguents, it would become red and blistered.

There was an assortment of scented soaps and lotions provided of which she made lavish use, finally drying herself with the enormous Turkish towel, with which she had also been provided. The luxury of her surroundings was something which she was heartily enjoying, it almost compensated for the annoyance caused by Giulio. She had all too frequently had to stay at cheap hotels and pensions where the appointments left much to be desired, though now that she was earning a big salary, she could afford better conditions.

The hotel in Rome had been comfortable, but there had been times when she had been taken upon photographic expeditions to remote places where even the best accommodation was primitive. There had been an occasion when she had been required to display Fair Isle sweaters in their native setting, and had had to spend two nights in a crofter's hut owing to a breakdown in transport. Mario had little idea of what hardships she had often met with, and had disbelieved her when she had hinted at them. She ought to have told him that during her teenage years on the farm she had learned to milk and had even driven the tractor, but he would have thought she was romancing.

She looked at her smooth hands with their pink-tipped

oval nails. She took infinite care of them, for they were part of her stock in trade. She had often been engaged to model where hands only were required, and one photographer had told her she had the most exquisite hands he had ever seen. They certainly did not look as if they had ever performed a menial task, but she was not incompetent, she could be as domesticated as any woman, but she always wore gloves for such chores.

She remembered Mario's brown hands, and what they had suggested to her. Idly she put her own fingers on either side of her waist, and went hot all over as she realised whence her thoughts were tending.

Damn him, she thought, why does he obsess me so? With an effort, she thrust him out of her thoughts, and wrapping herself in a silk robe proceeded to brush her hair vigorously.

Green Venetian blinds shut out the sunshine and her room was lit with cool emerald light, which had the effect of being under water. She had no wish to hurry back to join the noisy crowd outside.

Footsteps and a murmur of voices sounded from the terrace. The way to the private car park led past her window, and someone, probably Mario, was about to depart.

On sudden impulse, Lorena went to the blind, and adjusted the slats so that she could peer between them.

Mario was walking by with the Riccis. The Signora was teetering along on high-heeled sandals, and her broad face was wreathed in delighted smiles, for Mario was obviously saying gallant things to her, which seemed to please her husband, for he was smiling indulgently. Mario, she noticed, moved with feline grace, lithely and silently, a snow leopard, and like the leopard, fierce and unpredictable.

At the end of the terrace they halted, and Lorena heard Signora Ricci call:

'*Arrivederci, signor*, we will see you then for dinner.'

Her husband chuckled as he added: 'We will make you a

convert to the *dolce vita* yet!'

What Mario replied, she could not hear, but he turned back to wave, and she saw the sardonic smile on his face. Why was he coming, she wondered, when he so obviously despised the company he would meet? It was hardly fair to accept the Riccis' hospitality merely to sneer at their guests. She felt a little quiver of excited anticipation as she realised that she would meet him again, but naturally he would be appropriated by his hostess, and she hoped, or more correctly, she assured herself that she hoped, she would escape his notice.

But before dinner there was lunch and the long, hot afternoon.

Guessing that most of the party would be wearing beach wear, she perversely selected a pale green shift which covered her from neck to knees, and even had short sleeves. Her hair she did in two braids, one over each shoulder. The effect was that of an unsophisticated schoolgirl and created a stir when she appeared for the pre-lunch cocktail.

She encountered her hostess on her way to the terrace and the Signora gave her a beaming smile.

'Charming, *cara*,' she said in her heavily accented English. 'I like to see the sweet simplicity—so girlish, so demure.'

Lorena smiled and passed on to encounter Venetia's raised eyebrows and Marie-Céleste's look of scorn.

As she had surmised, most of the women were in bikinis, covered by beach wraps, which fell apart at the slightest movement. There was a fine display of tanned limbs, both male and female. Venetia's wrap was rainbow-hued and her hair poured over her shoulders like liquid flame. Marie-Céleste wore scanty scarlet, but her black head was neatly coiffured. She looked Lorena up and down and drawled:

'Surely, *mon amie*, you are very hot in a dress?'

'On the contrary, I find a dress fresh and cool,' Lorena returned, and amidst the medley of colours, she looked like

27

a waterlily in a bed of poppies.

Giulio brought her a sherry and regarded her with disapproval.

'Why do you cover your so beautiful body?' he asked. 'It cannot be that you are ashamed of it.'

It was mainly upon his account that she had put it on; she hated his appraising glances.

'Women are supposed to be mysterious,' she retorted. 'There's nothing mysterious about nudity.'

'You are a mystery to me,' he informed her. 'But one which I am determined to unravel.'

'It's not worth your while,' she told him meaningly.

He shrugged his shoulders and again said: '*Chi lo sa?*'

Signora Ricci rapped on a table with a spoon for attention.

'*Amici*, I have news for you,' she cried, beaming. 'The illustrious Signor Marescu will dine with us tonight.'

A ripple of excitement ran through the girls. Lorena was not the only one who had noticed Mario's striking personality.

Giulio muttered: 'What is so remarkable about him? He does not possess the half of what I do.'

Venetia laughed mockingly. 'You should hold aloof more, Giulio, then you would be more valued. Signora Ricci is triumphant because the elusive gentleman is so hard to capture.'

'Ah, it is always more exciting to hunt the one who flees,' Giulio agreed, with his eyes upon Lorena.

Marie-Céleste said: 'The satanic *monsieur*? Is he then of such great importance in this country?'

'Nobody in Sardinia is of importance,' Giulio said nastily. 'It is only a small island, though it has some good beaches. Marescu may be interested in its administration, I wouldn't know; administration of any sort bores me.' He lifted the glass of whisky he was holding. 'Here's to the gay life and a lovely woman!' He downed it at a gulp. 'And may she soon prove accessible,' he whispered to Lorena.

She shrank from his spirits-laden breath and longed to slap his face.

'That she never will be,' she said tersely.

He gave her an ugly glance and turned his attention to Venetia, who began to flirt with him outrageously. Lorena hoped fervently that her friend would succeed in detaching his interest from herself, though even if he were as rich as Croesus she could not understand how any girl could tolerate him.

During lunch, Lorena was filled with an unusual restlessness, which she would not confess to herself was caused by the prospect of encountering Mario again. She admitted that she found his company stimulating, even while he was planting his barbed darts, and assured herself that she was not likely to have much of that with so many other distractions.

Seeking a diversion, she threw out hints that she would like to explore Gallura, the division which included the Costa Smeralda, remarking that she had heard there were weird and wonderful rock formations to be seen there, but nobody rose.

Venetia said: 'We came to play and relax, not to get all hot and dusty rushing about sightseeing.'

'It's much pleasanter by the sea,' someone else pointed out. 'You can't be serious about wanting to see a lot of ugly rocks.'

Giulio, who had overheard and never missed a trick, promptly offered his escort, and Lorena had to pretend she had changed her mind, saying perhaps after all it would be too hot, and Signor Ricci told them he was planning a yacht trip in the near future, which, though it sounded pleasant, did nothing to alleviate Lorena's present restlessness.

It was too hot to swim after lunch, and she retired disconsolately to her room with a book. The story contained a dark, dashing hero, whom she kept identifying with Mario, finally flinging it across the room, disgusted both with it and her own silliness.

There was no formality about dressing for dinner, some of the girls liked to show off their long décolleté gowns, a few of the older men put on white dinner jackets, but the younger ones appeared in casual, often freakish costumes.

Lorena, for Mario's benefit, though she would not admit to herself that he was motivating her, chose a black evening dress which left her shoulders and a portion of her back bare. It had a long, full skirt, that fell in soft folds about her, moulding her hips. She twisted her hair about her head in a shining helmet, and made up her face with care. She had looked hot and dishevelled when she had come off the tennis court and she wanted to appear groomed and sophisticated. The black dress showed up the extreme fairness of her skin, and she was pleased with her appearance.

When she came into the lounge, she drew every male eye, for she eclipsed even Venetia's startling beauty, possessing a fragility and delicacy of feature which was more appealing than the red-haired girl's more blatant charms, but she was quite unaware of the sensation she was creating, for she was only interested in Mario's reaction.

He had arrived earlier in the evening, immaculate in evening dress, which contrasted favourably with the untidy look of many of the other men. She saw him staring at her, and he made a movement towards her, but Signora Ricci held his arm possessively.

'Tonight, *signor*, as your hostess, I claim your attention.'

There was no allocation of dinner partners; everyone endeavoured to sit beside the flame of the moment. Lorena found herself between Giulio and a boy who was regarding her with dazzled eyes. Mario was opposite to her, a little to one side. Down the length of the table were vases of flowers, exotic orchids from the Riccis' hothouses, but in spite of the floral barrier, Lorena was visible to him, and she soon became aware that he was watching her closely while he inclined an ear to Signora Ricci's platitudinous chat. His expression was one of stern disapproval, and that spurred her on to flirting shamelessly with the handsome boy beside her, and even Giulio received some of her smiles.

She resented the way in which Mario was daring to censure her, and even more so her own reactions to him. She was defying not only him but herself.

Since he had cast her in the role of adventuress, she would play the part, and if her behaviour antagonised him further, so much the better. Dimly she was aware that he presented a threat to her carefully preserved serenity. No man could be more important to her than her career, it was a life which she enjoyed and she was not prepared to let any will-o'-the-wisp of love interfere with her concentration upon it, though she suspected that what Mario was awakening in her was only the first stirrings of sex.

He had expressed his contempt for her work, considering that she looked upon it as a method to exploit her charms, but then the Latin male was never complaisant about working girls whatever their occupation. He still thought a woman's place was in the home, ministering to her husband and children, although the economic situation was causing him to grudgingly revise his views. Mario, of course, still held the old-fashioned one; he would like to see her chaperoned and restricted until some member of his sex chose her to run his home and submit to his domination.

She flashed a provocative glance at him, while her companion softly stroked her bare arm, and saw a smouldering fire in his eyes. Then Signora Ricci addressed some remark to him, tapping his sleeve with her pudgy fingers. He turned to her almost, it seemed, with relief, and Lorena's annoyance grew. What concern of his was it how she behaved? He had no right to look at her with such ... fury was it? ... in his gaze. Giulio on her other side was smouldering too, incensed by the liberties which she was allowing to the young man. The atmosphere about her was charged with electricity.

Lorena drank rather more of the sweet white, Moscata del Tempi, than was normal for her to allay her sensation of growing tension and became slightly reckless. The long meal was composed of many alternative dishes, starting with fish soup. Lorena chose the Sardo confections, pasta di Sardo, a special member of the macaroni family, and a dish composed of small semi-dumplings flavoured with sheep's milk cheese and coloured with saffron, served with a piquante sauce. There was roast kid for those who preferred it, lobster, and many forms of sardines. The sweet course was more ordinary, consisting of ice cream confections, and there was an abundance of hothouse fruit, including out-of-season strawberries.

Dancing followed, and Lorena wondered with mingled excitement and apprehension if Mario would ask her to dance with him. Mostly tangos and foxtrots were played on the powerful stereogram in preference to the more modern gymnastics. She danced once with Giulio, unable to avoid his importunities, and then her dinner partner, who, emboldened by encouragement she had given him, took full advantage of the opportunities the tango presented, pressing her close to him, and putting his cheek against hers. She did not notice his proximity, being absorbed in watching Mario, who had danced sedately with his hostess, and then, to her slight chagrin, with Marie-Céleste. The French girl's expression was almost comical as she yielded to the arms of her satanic *monsieur*; it was a mingling of gratification and awe. Then to Lorena's disappointment he disappeared, but whether alone or accompanied, she did not know. Then she became aware of the liberties her partner was taking and rebuked him sharply.

As the evening progressed, the anticipation engendered by Mario's presence died away to be succeeded by depression. Her fastidiousness revolted against the amorous glances cast upon her and the whole pleasure-loving, thoughtless crowd, and most especially from Giulio, who was trying to monopolise her. Murmuring an excuse that she wanted to powder her nose, she managed to give him the slip and escaped to her room. She opened her window to let in the cool night air. Moonlight flooded the terrace, which at that point seemed to be deserted. Picking up a flimsy shawl, she draped it over her shoulders, opened the catch of the french window, and stole out on to the terrace. She turned towards the deserted car park and crept down on to the beach.

The moon was nearing its full, throwing a white path across the calm sea, indigo-coloured bordered with creamy lace; the sand was an ivory waste. Lorena walked hurriedly until she was well away from the villa, then, satisfied that no one had followed her, she sat down on a dry rock and looked towards the land.

Lights and music came from the various hotels and villas, the former looking like great galleons against the purple sky, but beyond was the interior, mysterious, unknown, the real Sardinia and the mountains from which Mario had said he had come.

She would very much like to explore it, and after all, why should she not? She might never come this way again. She could hire a car, she was an expert driver, and there must be a car hire service nearby, and escape into the country on her own. It could be done with a little ingenuity—considerable ingenuity if she were to circumvent Giulio—and it would be a relief to get away for a while, if only for one long day.

Lost in her thoughts, she was startled by the sound of a foot striking a rock behind her, and turned swiftly to face the intruder, afraid that Giulio had tracked her down, but the man looking down at her was Mario. He had come upon her with his soundless cat-like tread, and she had been unaware of his approach. He stood with his back to the moon, his face in shadow above his white dinner jacket, a slightly menacing figure, and her heartbeat accelerated.

'All alone?' he asked, 'or have I intruded upon an assignment?'

'No, I'm not expecting anybody. I was tired of the heat and noise and I wanted to be by myself,' she explained hurriedly, thinking he was the last person she had expected to follow her.

'Is that a hint to take myself off?' he asked.

'I will endeavour to endure your company if you can endure mine,' she said demurely.

'H'm, mutual tolerance? You are not very encouraging, but you should not wander so far afield alone without a man to protect you.'

'Are your countrymen then such ruffians?'

'They are always courteous to women. It is not they who might embarrass you but the riff-raff that has been imported.'

A reflection upon her associates, she thought, as she said: 'Then it would be quite safe to take a trip alone into the interior?'

'That depends,' he said doubtfully. 'But surely you have no need to go alone? Haven't you plenty of cavaliers who would be pleased to escort you?'

'None that I fancy.'

'You surprise me. May I sit down?' Without waiting for her permission he seated himself on the rock beside her. Instinctively she moved further away. Noticing her action, he said proudly:

'I have no intention of touching you, though you did not seem to mind the attentions of your dinner partner.'

Lorena had the grace to look ashamed. Anxious to change the subject, she asked quickly:

'Why did you come after me?'

'It wasn't intentional. I too wearied of the racket and came out for a stroll on the beach. I saw your footsteps in

34

the sand, and was intrigued; there was only one spoor, normally there are two. Then I caught sight of you with the moonlight silvering your hair, like a siren sitting on your rock, and I was irresistibly drawn to you. The Lorelei has nothing on you. Are you quite human, *signorina*?'

'What an absurd question! Of course I am.'

'But like those enchantresses of old you have no heart?'

The organ in question was making its presence felt in Lorena's breast; the moonlight and the man's magnetic personality was affecting her strangely, but she managed to answer coolly:

'I hope I have my full complement of natural attributes.'

He laughed. 'What a prosaic response to my flights of fancy! Do you mind if I smoke?'

'Not at all.' He took out his case and lit a cheroot; the flame from his lighter illuminated his face. There was something a little demonic about it, she thought, with its tilted dark brows, and satirical mouth, crowned by his thick black hair. If she were the water nymph of legend, he could have posed for Pan, the god of the woods; there was something untamed about him. Involuntarily she glanced at his ears, half expecting to discover they were pointed, but they were flat and ordinarily shaped, set close to his head.

'I wonder Signora Ricci let you escape,' she said with a hint of malice.

He smiled. 'I think she found the pace too hot for her; she has retired to rest. Do you imagine that it was on her account that I came here tonight?'

'She asked you, and I don't flatter myself it was upon mine.'

'But of course, *signorina*,' he returned with mock gallantry. 'I couldn't resist your lure. Actually I had business to discuss with Ricci.'

'That you did this morning. It didn't entail coming to dinner, did it?'

'It is as well to foster friendly relations—besides, am I

not allowed some relaxation?'

'I thought you didn't like the company.'

'It is always amusing to watch the antics of aliens,' he retorted airily, and Lorena wilted. So she had contributed to his entertainment by her 'antics', for it was she whom he had been watching through dinner, though he had not looked amused by her behaviour but censorious.

'I think I should return,' she said frostily.

'Please don't go yet. I want to know why you are desirious of making a solitary expedition into the hinterland.'

She relented, finding herself oddly loath to leave him.

'I want to see the real country without distractions,' she told him. 'Are there any places which I should avoid? I have heard there are bandits?'

'You are unlikely to encounter any. The outlaws hide in the Barbagia, the wild country surrounding the Gennargentu, and you would be unable to penetrate their hideout.'

'So they really do exist and aren't just a myth to frighten adventurous travellers?'

'*Si*, they exist,' he said sombrely. He looked away across the moonlit sea. 'Most of them are men who have killed in a vendetta.'

She stared incredulously at his profile, the fine features of which were etched against the silvery water.

'But ... but isn't that a thing of the past?' she asked. 'I mean, nowadays with police and proper control, hasn't it been stamped out?'

'Not entirely. It still operates in the Mediterranean islands, especially in Sicily. I would gladly see it eradicated, for it has decimated many of our best families, but so long as the idea persists that a man must in honour avenge his kin himself, it is difficult. Proceedings are wrapped in secrecy, for no one will help the *carabinieri* to catch the offenders. All enquiries are met with silence.'

Lorena glanced along the coastline at the hotels and all the signs of twentieth-century living. The information that blood feuds could continue amid such modern innovations was unbelievable. She turned her gaze back to the man beside her. Outwardly, in his perfectly fitting dinner clothes, he was a suave and sophisticated man of the world, but she was dimly aware that his outward seeming was only a veneer laid over the elemental forces in the depths of his nature, as the modern hotels were only excrescences upon the unchanging rocks of Arachenza. Sardinia had been called the unconquered island, for though various nations had sought to overrun it, and many savage wars had ravaged it, its core had never been subdued.

In the heart of its mountains still lived the fierce vindictive spirit of its progenitors, who believed that a life must be paid for a life, and Mario had told her he came from the mountains. Upon their first meeting she had been intrigued by the suggestion of restrained passion about his personality, and if he were provoked beyond his control, she could well imagine that he would be as primitive as his forebears. Again she thought of a leashed leopard, and the leopard is the fiercest and most cruel of the big cats.

He seemed lost in reverie, her presence forgotten; his face had become bleak. The gentle wash of the wavelets on the beach sounded loud in the stillness. She said uncertainly:

'But you yourself cannot condone such a custom?'

He recalled himself from wherever it was his thoughts had led him, and turned to her with a swift smile.

'Of course I don't. I believe in law and order, and I hope education and better living standards will finally eradicate the vendetta.' His eyes went past her, with a brooding look. 'However, one cannot wholly ignore one's heritage. Traditions die hard. I own land in the hills. If a near relative of mine were involved, and instead of avenging him personally I called in the police, my peasantry would spit upon me.'

She glimpsed a vision of an earlier age, purposeful men among the mountains motivated by revenge. The dark, inscrutable man beside her would be capable of such a hunt, and concealing his actions with secrecy—the predator seeking his prey. The old traditions were at war in him with a modern education.

Yet because she had lived all her life among ultra-civilised people, she was fascinated by the elemental male in him and did not wholly recoil from this flight of fancy. Mario, she thought, was a bit of an anachronism. He wanted to keep his women in purdah, and he did not entirely repudiate his right to destroy his enemies. Then her common sense reasserted itself. Whatever he was and whatever he did could not affect her. This was only a chance meeting, and after tonight they would each go their several ways.

'But your peasants are only ignorant people,' she said lightly. 'You should let them spit.'

He smiled satirically. 'You are not a Sard, so how could you understand? But you are not likely to encounter the *banditti*. However, there are other dangers, and I do not think you would be wise to travel about alone.'

'Oh, nonsense,' she said impatiently. 'I read a travel book by a woman who went everywhere on the island and found everybody most happy to help her.'

'I do not suppose she looked like you do.'

His nostrils flared slightly, and she turned her head away, unable to meet the ardent look in his eyes. He laughed softly, and added drily: 'Perhaps what you really mean is that you want to keep a secret tryst in the hills?'

'Nothing of the sort!' She was incensed. 'Do you think I can't take an interest in anything except men?'

'Yes,' he affirmed. 'I expect you to run true to form.'

'The form you've prescribed for me?'

'To which you have admitted.'

She was silent, going over in her mind what she could remember of her previous conversations with him. Outstanding was her declaration on the plane that she would only settle for ten thousand a year. A stupid thing to have said, and she had not expected him to take it seriously, as he had done. But then she had not thought she would ever meet him again.

The fragrant smell from his cheroot mingled with the faint aromatic scent of herbs wafted seawards by the land breeze, which stirred the tendrils of her hair. As if he had read her thought, he remarked casually:

'I imagine Giulio's income reaches the stipulated sum, and you seem to be making the running with him. Wouldn't it be an error of tactics to vanish into the interior at this stage? Or do you hope that he will pursue you? If you are aiming to get him alone in some isolated spot, you might do well to reflect that he may not consider it is necessary to marry you, however compromised you may be.'

'I'm not scheming to trap Giulio, if that's what you mean,' she cried indignantly. He merely smiled disbelievingly, and she looked at him curiously. 'If you compromised a girl, even inadvertently, would you feel bound to marry her?'

'It would be the honourable thing to do,' he returned gravely.

So his notions with regard to women were, as she had suspected, old-fashioned; he was, she thought, full of contradictions, combining chivalry with savage ruthlessness. Daringly she enquired:

'Even if she were a calculating minx like myself?'

'That rather depends upon the circumstances. If a scandal was threatened, certainly; you see, my honour would be involved as well as hers.'

'Then I wonder you aren't afraid to be alone with me now. I might try to make capital out of the situation,' and she glanced at him provocatively.

He smiled sardonically. 'You forget my income comes nowhere near your minimum, so I know I am in no danger from you.'

His gaze returned to the sea, while she studied his profile. The finely moulded features were like those on a Greek coin. Silence fell between them, broken only by the whisper of the wavelets on the sand. Lorena was full of regret, for instinctively she felt that Mario possessed an integrity which her other associates lacked, and his misconceptions regarding herself were causing her an unexpected pain. Yet she had wilfully fed those misconceptions and she doubted if anything that she could say now would change his opinion of her.

She sighed, and he turned his head to look at her. The shawl had slipped from her shoulders and her neck and arms were alabaster in the white light, her eyes wide and appealing.

'What an appearance of sweet innocence you can put on when you choose,' he said roughly. 'If he didn't know otherwise, how easily you would hoodwink a man. Almost I could....' He broke off his sentence and threw his half smoked cheroot away with a savage gesture.

'Almost you could ... what?' Lorena asked softly.

'Nothing. I am not a green boy to be deceived by a woman's wiles, so it is useless to practise them on me.'

He was openly sneering at her now, although she was aware of an undercurrent, as if he were trying to blacken her in his estimation to protect himself against her influence, but such a supposition was humiliating, and whatever was motivating him, she had taken enough from him for one evening.

She rose to her feet, drawing her shawl closely about her, and said coldly:

'You seem to take a mean satisfaction in cheapening me, but may I point out that you don't really know me at all, and I don't suppose you ever will.'

'Oh, I know you very well,' he retorted. 'Your type is all too obvious and very prevalent in places like the Costa Smeralda.'

40

She did not deign to respond to that quip.

'I'm going back,' she announced.

He rose to his feet and she added quickly: 'I would prefer that you don't accompany me.'

Rather to her chagrin, he took her at her word, sitting down again upon the rock.

'*Buona notta, signorina,*' he said, 'and incidentally, if you do go to the hills, you may gain some experience of real life in the raw, which would be a change for you.'

'I don't doubt I can cope,' she retorted. 'Goodnight and goodbye, *signor*. We are unlikely to meet again.'

'Most unlikely,' he agreed, and proceeded to light another cheroot.

Reluctantly she went across the silver sand, resisting a strong desire to look back at him. Mario continued to smoke without moving, but his eyes followed her slight black figure until she was out of sight.

That night Lorena lay sleepless upon her luxurious bed with its pink silk sheets and downy quilt, going over and over her conversation with Mario in endless repetition. She had been deeply incensed by many of his remarks and not a little wounded by others, but she was too fair-minded not to admit that she had asked for them.

She knew perfectly well that in Latin countries girls belonging to respectable families who were unmarried were still carefully guarded and free exchanges with young men were frowned upon. Mario in his judgment of her was only following the old conventions. She had been suspect from the moment when he had overheard Venetia's unfortunate remark. Her job was also against her; as her friend had said, Italian mamas would not hear of their daughters appearing as fashion models, and probably in a backward society like Sardinia's, the prejudice was even stronger. When he came to visit the Riccis, he had found her apparently upon good terms with Giulio, whom he had recommended to her as an exceptionally rich bachelor, so he had some excuse for his snide remarks, though in retrospect she found them even more painful.

It would be wonderful if he had offered to escort her upon her trip round the island, he knew it and its people and would have been a mine of information, though some of it, like his account of the vendetta, was slightly sinister. That took her thoughts into another channel. Was he really capable of shooting a man in cold blood to fulfil the *lex talionis*? she wondered, and came to the conclusion that Mario would be capable of anything in pursuit of his strange notions of honour.

Somewhere in the small hours, she admitted to herself frankly that the man fascinated her and she was more than sorry that their acquaintanceship had ended. She began to weave daydreams in which some unlikely happening occurred during which Mario was forced to reconsider his false assessment of her.

Finally, as dawn was stealing over the countryside, she fell into a troubled sleep and dreamed that she was being stalked by a hunting leopard with a human face, the face of Mario Marescu.

CHAPTER THREE

THE house party continued in a whirl of gaiety, rather forced gaiety at times, it seemed to Lorena. It lasted from the morning swim until long past midnight, when the dancing ended. The second day was a replica of the first.

Still intent upon taking a solitary expedition into the hinterland, Lorena ascertained that she could hire a car in Olbia, a town not far distant, and booked one over the telephone for the middle of the week.

Meanwhile she joined energetically in all the fun and games, striving to drive the memory of Mario out of her mind. She politely, but firmly indicated to the younger men of the party that she was not available for necking sessions. They were not offended, there were others more amenable, and laughed at her for being an ice maiden.

The older men were less obvious, and for the most part harmless, merely wanting a confidante to listen to their troubles, but much to her disgust, and in spite of all her efforts to avoid him, she was always finding herself being paired with Giulio.

On the third day, the one before that upon which she planned to slip off on her own to visit the mountains, an expedition was arranged to go by yacht down the coast to visit the Grotta del Bue Marino. It was a sunny, windless day, which was unusual; there was normally a breeze, if not actually a wind, but that did not affect the Riccis' yacht, which was driven by a diesel engine.

'The sails are only for ornament,' one young man remarked with disgust, since he knew something about sailing.

On that particular morning they were furled.

Giulio, to Lorena's relief, did not come on board. He

accompanied the yacht in his powerful motor boat, racing past it and heading out to sea, to return in a swirl of spray and smug satisfaction.

'Hateful creature!' Lorena said to Venetia, as they leaned over the rail on deck watching this performance. 'Almost I could wish he would drown himself.'

Venetia gave her a side-long look.

'My dear, he's awfully rich, and he's fallen for you hook, line and sinker. Playing hard to get has made him all the keener. He'll end by asking you to marry him.'

Lorena shuddered. 'Ven, I can't bear him. He's slimy.'

'But think, dear, of all he can give you. He's got a house in Rome, a villa on the Riviera, a flat in Paris. You'll have jewels, furs, cars, anything you want. Surely that's worth a little ... slime?'

Venetia had evidently being checking up upon Giulio's assets.

'Not to me it isn't,' Lorena said firmly. 'I couldn't marry a man I loathed.'

Venetia smiled wisely. 'It often starts with a little aversion, and I understand all husbands are much the same after the first year.'

'Don't be such a cynic,' Lorena told her. 'Let's talk of something else. Are those porpoises?' and she pointed to a line of dark leaping shapes.

'Could be.' Venetia was uninterested. She looked at her friend shrewdly. 'You haven't fallen for that forbidding-looking Sard, have you? I saw him looking at you when he visited us, but he's no use to you. Probably up to his neck in some family vendetta, and though he looks affluent, nobody knows where he makes his money. Bootlegging, I shouldn't wonder. You'd best steer clear of him.'

'I intend to,' Lorena returned, trying not to look conscious. 'But I shan't be seeing him again, and there are things much more important to me than matrimony.'

'Nothing is more important than matrimony,' Venetia

44

announced with a twinkle in her brown eyes. 'It means security and money to spend if you pick the right guy. If you married Giulio, you could do such a lot for your friends; lovely places to stay, and he must have a lot of rich and influential pals.'

Lorena only laughed.

'I'm afraid I couldn't consider marrying Giulio simply to provide you with holiday homes and opportunities,' she said lightly. 'Sorry to have to disappoint you.'

Venetia looked a little peeved.

'You're a starry-eyed romantic,' she grumbled. 'It's a darned sight more practical to be a cynic like me. But perhaps you'll come to your senses before this week is out.'

'I've never left them,' Lorena assured her. 'Giulio just isn't possible, Venetia.'

Venetia gave her a cunning glance, but said no more.

The yacht anchored in the Golfo di Orosei and Giulio's boat was used to ferry its passengers ashore to the small seaport where lunch had been prepared for them. Several hotels were grouped round the little town, interspersed by private villas. Beetling cliffs surrounded the bay, fringed with scrub and small oaks. The coast was inundated with solitary little bays containing tempting stretches of white sand, and in places, extraordinary striations of rock swirled this way and that down to the water's edge in a variety of colours.

They ate in the open air, fresh lobster and salad washed down by a dry white wine which was made in the country. The meal was concluded with magnificent ripe peaches.

Afterwards, Lorena joined those members of the party who wished to see the Grotto, being ferried thither in Giulio's motor launch. Since there were half a dozen of them and Giulio was busy with the controls, he could not pester her.

The boat slipped in under an overhanging rock and a guide was waiting to escort them, carrying lanterns and torches. From the entrance, a railed path led to the inner caves.

A river led off to the left, a freshwater stream which ran down through the caverns. The way opened up through chambers filled with stalactites and stalagmites in unbelievable size and colours. Obsidian crystals shining white on rose gold rock, alabaster, pink, white and yellow, and many-hued quartz. It was an Ali Baba's cave of living jewels.

In the furthest cave of all, seals were supposed to live, emerging at night and dawn to feed. They were the only seals existing in the Mediterranean and were protected by law, and it was they who gave the Grotto its name—the Seals' Cave. The guide said he had heard them, but had never actually seen them.

Lorena could have willingly explored the whole of the galleries, extending for nearly five kilometres. The place fascinated her, but her companions soon began to flag, their interest waning. Reluctantly she followed them back to where the launch was moored. Giulio, to her great relief, had stayed with it.

Looking at the inviting little bays below the cliffs, where the water was so clear that every ripple in the sand, every shell and weed was visible below its surface, Giulio suggested landing for a swim. He would, he said, fetch anyone else who cared to join them.

Anticipating something of the sort, Lorena carried her bikini and a towel in a beach bag. Rocks gave plenty of cover and soon she was swimming in the fresh, cool waters of the bay.

Giulio returned with several passengers and a supply of drinks. After the swim, they all lay on the sand, basking in the sun, while the sea turned violet blue in the afternoon light.

Tired with her long walk through the galleries, Lorena fell asleep.

She awoke with a sense of chill to find that she was lying in the shade and a breeze was blowing. The sea looked dark and the cliff behind her threw a lengthening ominous shadow over the beach. She looked round and found that she was alone. Sitting up, alarmed, she drew her towel over her shoulders and peered out into the bay. The yacht should have been visible in the distance, but it was no longer there. Then to her relief she saw the shape of the motor boat in the lee of a rock, but relief was followed by apprehension as Giulio came towards her.

'I've been asleep,' she remarked childishly. 'Where are the others?'

'All gone home,' he told her. 'They soon had enough of this place, but you were sleeping so peacefully, we were loath to disturb you—at least your friend Venetia was. I told her I would come back to fetch you after I had put the others aboard the yacht.'

She realised with horror that she was quite alone with him, and was furious with Venetia for her treachery. She had deliberately engineered the situation.

'Let's go, then,' she said trying to speak calmly. 'It's getting cold here.'

'But first you will pay for your passage, *si*?' he said slyly. 'Always you give me the cold shoulder, but now, if you want to go home, you will have to be nice to me.'

He sidled up to her and put a claw-like hand upon her arm. Lorena froze with disgust and shook it off as if it had been a noxious insect.

'I'd rather walk the whole way back than go with you! Leave me alone. I loathe you!'

Had she been less revolted by his touch, she would have realised that she was unwise to antagonise him when he was her only means of leaving the place, but she could not bring herself to cajole him.

An evil glint came into his eyes and he picked up her beach bag into which she had put her clothes when she disrobed.

'Please give me my bag,' she said anxiously.

'Only if you pay ransom for it.' She recoiled and he added suavely:

'Perhaps you will change your tune after an hour or so's reflection. You are hardly suitably dressed for a long walk, *signorina*, nor will you find it easy to get out of this cove. *Arrivederci* for now, and perhaps when I return you will greet me a little more kindly.'

He ran back to his boat, threw her bag on board and followed it himself. The chug-chug of the engine came to her over the sands, as he swept out of the bay.

Lorena looked about her. Above her rose the sheer cliff, grim and forbidding. On either side rocks ran out into the sea. The little bay, so inviting in the sunlight, looked sinister in shadow. It might be hours, even days, before anyone came to it.

She ran down to the water's edge, for it seemed that only by swimming could she escape, for escape she must before Giulio returned. She wondered how far it was to the seaport where they had lunched. There was not a light showing anywhere and dusk was falling. She dropped into the sea and swam in the direction of the port, but she was cold and tired, and the current was against her. Rounding a point of striated rock, she was swept into another little cove and then, to her intense relief, she saw a light.

Swimming towards it, she saw it was the riding light of a small ship moored close into a ledge of rock which formed a natural landing stage with deep water below it. Some fisherman's smack, she thought, but she would prefer fishermen to Giulio. She swam up to the dark bulk and called, but the ship appeared to be deserted.

She looked along the serrated coast, and far away, too far for her to swim, was a twinkle of lights. There seemed to be no other refuge except this boat, but how was she to get aboard it?

She swam round it, aware her strength was failing, and found beyond it a jumble of rocks which were not unscaleable. Wearily she pulled herself out of the water and clambered back towards the ship, guided by the faint glimmer of light from its masthead. It had become for her a beacon of hope, a promise of human presences in a rather frightening wilderness of rock and sand.

At length she gained the ledge of rock which formed a natural quay, and which was smooth and level under her bare feet. Scratched and bruised from her climb, she pattered along it, until she discovered a plank set like a gangway on to the ship's deck. Gingerly she ran across it, for it was narrow, and looked around. There was no sign of anybody on board. The ship, actually it was a small cutter, rocked gently at anchor. There was a cabin amidships, its hatch open. She climbed the coaming into the cockpit and shouted down:

'Ahoy there!'

At least she tried to shout, but her voice sounded pitifully weak and thin. Warm air ascended through the hatchway, and she was shivering with weariness and exposure. Almost without thought, except that here was shelter, she clambered down the few ladderlike steps of the companionway into the cabin.

A lantern swung from the ceiling showing her two bunks along either side, with a narrow table down the middle. Inside, to her right, was the galley, with a Primus stove and various cooking pots. A sliding door led forward to the fo'c'sle and was half open.

She sat down on the bunk, thankful that it was warm, the sun-drenched deck had retained some heat. She wondered how she could account for her presence when the crew appeared, as presumably it would do eventually.

It was possible that she could persuade the fishermen to land her at Arachenza with the promise of a reward, but would they understand Italian, for she could not speak the Sardo dialect? Probably enough to comprehend her request. Someone might even have a few words of English.

She heard with some trepidation the sound of heavy foot-steps overhead. The crew was coming aboard. Instinctively she looked about her for somewhere to hide, assailed by sudden panic. The fo'c'sle presented a tempting hideout. Yielding to her unreasoning fear, she slipped into it.

It was quite dark inside, the forehatch being closed, and she collided with several unidentifiable objects, causing some noise. She held her breath, listening, but no one on deck seemed to have heard anything. Cautiously she turned round so that she could see the interior of the cabin through the half open door.

From the sounds above her head she surmised that the boat was casting off, and her panic subsided. Now she must decide what she would say when she was discovered. Her situation did not greatly perturb her, and she would rather face an army of fishermen than contend with Giulio. There was something about him which made her flesh crawl, as some people are affected by spiders.

She would explain that she had been swimming and had been carried away by the current, and if it were incon-venient to land her on the Costa Smeralda tonight, she was willing to stay aboard until morning. She wished that she was more clothed, but girls in bikinis must be a familiar sight along that coast.

A steady chug-chug indicated that the boat possessed an auxiliary engine. The water rippled along the side of the ship, then, as it gained the open sea, the engine was cut out and the motion became more pronounced as the breeze filled the sails.

She heard footsteps and voices descending the com-panionway. Youthful tones exclaimed in Italian:

'So that's the last of Sardegna. *Dio*, I could do with a drink!'

Another voice answered, and it seemed vaguely familiar.

'There's wine in the galley, but go easy on it, Guido my boy. You have a long journey in front of you, and we have a

50

lot of sailing to do before you have finished even the first
leg.'

Words with their implication of a long trip which were
not very reassuring to the stowaway.

Two men came into the cabin and seemed to fill its small
space with their bulk. Involuntarily Lorena stepped back,
and collided with something which gave out a metallic ring.

The man called Guido froze in the act of pouring out a
beaker of wine, exclaiming:

'*Dio mio*, what was that?'

His companion took a stride towards the fo'c'sle door,
pushed it wide open and shone a torch into the interior.

Summoning what boldness she could, Lorena prepared
for the confrontation, though at sight of the two dark figures, her courage had begun to ebb.

'So we have a stowaway,' the man drawled. 'Come out
and let us have a look at you.'

Reluctantly Lorena emerged from her refuge and found
herself face to face with Mario Marescu.

Oh, no, she thought, not him again! But it was very
definitely Mario, and with a rush of embarrassment, she
recalled his comments about her appearance in a bikini.
Now she was to display herself in that scanty garb. She
longed for the concealing comfort of slacks and shirt, but
they were unobtainable. Why, of all the boats at anchor
along the coast, had fate led her to seek refuge in his?

The other man, she was sure, was Mario's brother, they
were so alike, but Guido was slighter than Mario and his
face, particularly his mouth, betrayed weakness of character. Both were wearing dark sweaters and seamen's boots,
both had similar crops of dark hair and both had the same
ebony eyes under falcon's brows.

The light from the torch illuminated Lorena in a golden
glow, and shone on the silver-gilt of her hair. She had
shaken it forward to conceal as much of herself as possible.
Between its meshes, her wide eyes stared appealingly at

51

Mario.

Recovering from his surprise, he said mockingly:

'It is the siren from the Costa Smeralda! So we meet again, *signorina*.'

Hastily she stumbled into her explanation. She had swum further than she had intended; being cold and tired she had sought refuge aboard—the gangplank had invited her and she could not resist the warmth of the cabin.

Guido said anxiously: 'But what was Bruno doing to let you come on deck?' Both men had addressed her in English.

'Bruno was watching the landward path and our visitor has come from the sea,' Mario pointed out. 'It seems she has had a rough passage,' he added, glancing at her scratched legs.

'I did indeed,' she confirmed.

Her story had sounded thin and she did not think that either of them swallowed it.

'Very late at night to be swimming—alone,' Mario observed.

She could not meet the derision in his eyes, derision and something else.

Guido's black eyes sparkled a little maliciously, as he said in Italian:

'It seems your efforts to detach me from one female enchantress, Mario, have resulted in encountering another, and *dio*, this one could make a man break all the ten commandments!'

Mario gave him a warning glance.

'Your folly is no joking matter,' he said witheringly, 'and may well lead to serious consequences for us all. As for the Signorina, she is no concern of yours, and she may understand Italian.'

'I both understand and speak it,' Lorena told them in that tongue.

The man named Guido looked a little disconcerted, then

he laughed gaily and made her a little bow.

'Accomplished as well as beautiful! How sad that I am going far away and we meet only to part.'

'That is just as well,' Mario remarked drily. 'She is too expensive for you.'

Lorena stared at him angrily. 'You talk as if I were a man-eater,' she said heatedly. 'I'm not, you know.'

Mario merely shrugged his shoulders and smiled.

'I'm sorry if I'm inconveniencing you,' she went on more calmly. 'I thought this was a fishing vessel.'

'So it is,' Mario returned blandly. 'We often go out fishing.'

He had been studying her closely ever since she had come into the cabin, his eyes lingering on her slender, delicately formed limbs, the fine web of her hair. Now he noticed the glow in Guido's, and he went to one of the cupboards fixed above the berths, and extracting a rough towelling robe, thrust it towards Lorena.

'Please to cover yourself up before you completely demoralise my crew,' he said harshly.

Hastily Lorena grabbed it, donned it and tied the girdle firmly about her waist.

Guido said gleefully: 'I have yet to meet the girl who could demoralise old Bruno, though she might confirm his belief in mermaids. She is really beautiful, Mario. That hair....' He stretched out a brown hand to touch it and Mario slapped it down.

'*Basta!*' he snapped. 'Your amorous propensities have done enough damage already. The breeze seems to be freshening and you can go and help Bruno put on more sail. The sooner we reach our destination the better.'

Guido glanced wickedly at the other man.

'Should I leave you alone with her?' he queried. 'Are you equal to combating the wiles of a siren? She will entangle you in her silken web and drug your senses with the witchery of her embrace.'

Both Mario and Lorena coloured, she from embarrassment, he because Guido had guessed the trend of his thoughts.

'Don't talk rubbish, and do as you are told,' he said curtly. 'I must explain to the Signorina her situation, and I can do it more effectively without your interruptions.'

Guido looked at Lorena with commiseration. 'Poor mermaid,' he murmured. He went out reluctantly, and Mario closed the cabin door behind him, sliding the hatch across.

'Sit down,' he commanded, turning towards Lorena.

She sat down nervously on one of the bunks, drawing her wrap closely around her. Mario seated himself opposite to her, with the table between them, but the space was so narrow, he seemed to loom over her.

'I can't put into Arachenza now,' he said shortly. 'My errand tonight is urgent. You will have to reconcile yourself to being at sea until morning.'

'That's okay by me,' she told him. 'I'm in no hurry to return to the Costa Smeralda.'

He looked at her penetratingly.

'What really happened? Did your escort prove to be more than you could handle?' he asked bluntly.

To her annoyance, she could not control her blush, and he laughed mockingly. 'I am surprised you were unable to cope.'

As if impelled by an ungovernable impulse, he leaned forward across the table and grasped her hair on either side of her head, holding a handful in each brown fist.

'*Madonna mia*, I don't blame him,' he said softly. 'Hair like this is worth a king's ransom, soft as silk and the colour of ripe barley. Add to that eyes like the light of dawn and a skin resembling magnolia petals, while as for your mouth....' his gaze became fixed on its soft curves. 'Were you crazy to come among dark men, like the Sards? Don't you know what you do to us?'

'Surely you've seen a blonde woman before?' she asked

54

sharply, trying to control the excitement his touch and tone was causing her. She could feel his knuckles against her temples and the expression in his deep eyes was causing tremors to run up her spine. 'I gather I've butted in at an awkward moment,' she went on. 'Am I right in assuming there is something hush-hush about your expedition to-night?'

He gave her hair a sharp tug, which hurt, then releasing his hold of it, he leaned back, putting his hands into his trouser pockets, and stared up at the lantern.

'Maybe,' he admitted.

Lorena considered how she could turn the situation to her advantage. She did not want to rejoin Signor Ricci's house party. Giulio would still be there, and it was possible that she could make a bargain with Mario since she had unwittingly stumbled into what appeared to be a secret mission. She said quietly:

'For personal reasons I don't want to go back to Signor Ricci's, but I need my clothes and passport. If on our return I gave you a note for my friend Venetia....'

'Telling her to get in touch with the *carabinieri*?' he interrupted.

She looked at him doubtfully. 'You really are evading the law?'

'There is no law against midnight fishing, but perhaps you are contemplating laying a charge against me for kidnapping you?'

'Oh, don't be so absurd,' she exclaimed impatiently. 'I told you I was willing to stay the night.'

'Indeed?' he murmured significantly, while his fine mouth curled sardonically.

'Please don't try to twist my words. I merely thought that if you could ask Venetia to pack my things and give them to you, I needn't go back at all.'

'Why should I do this for you?'

'Because in return I will forget I ever saw you or your

boat tonight.'

'How kind of you,' he jeered. 'So you think I shall be returning to this coast tomorrow?'

She had taken it for granted, but now it occurred to her that his cutter, or whatever the boat was, could reach any port in the Mediterranean, it was quite large enough, and wherever he was going she would have to go too. The realisation was disquieting.

'Oh, dear, if you're not, that'll be very awkward,' she exclaimed. 'I need clothes before I can go ashore'—he grinned maddeningly—'and money. Could you make me a loan?'

'Could you repay it?'

'Of course I could, when I can get hold of my travellers' cheques.' She spoke with asperity, for she hated having to ask a favour of him, but she could not allow herself to be stranded at a strange port.

'Travellers cheques be damned!' He leaned across the table, his eyes glinting. 'The payment I would exact would be much less expensive and far more amusing.' Again he touched her hair. 'Presumably the ice maiden melts when it is expedient to do so.'

Alarmed, she shrank back from him. '*Signor!*' she protested.

He laughed merrily. 'You are unexpectedly naïve occasionally, *signorina*,' he told her. 'But I was only teasing you. For your comfort, know that I am not a bad, bold pirate with designs upon your person, nor have you stumbled upon a secret which will enable you to bargain for your silence.'

Like cloud after sunshine, sombreness settled on his face again.

'I shall be returning to Sardegna, but in my time, not in yours. Now I must go up on deck. You will be so good as to stay here below. It is necessary for both our sakes that neither Bruno nor anyone else should know of your presence

56

aboard, particularly as we shall be returning alone.'

She interrupted: 'But don't you consider I've no reputation to lose?' and hoped he would deny it.

'Harbouring you will not enhance mine,' he returned, to her vexation. He went on coolly: 'You must excuse me if I shut you in here, since I don't trust you not to make a sudden appearance on deck, if the inclination takes you, before Bruno and Guido have gone ashore. And I'm afraid you must stay in the dark.' He reached up and extinguished the lantern. 'I suggest you go to sleep.'

Lighting his way with his torch, he went out of the cabin, closing the door behind him, and shutting down the hatch. Lorena heard a bolt being drawn.

She was a prisoner below deck, the hatch battened down ... phrases from juvenile sea stories read in childhood recurred to her, and here she must stay until the crew had completed their business. She wondered what it could be, and in spite of Mario's denial, the thought of smuggling persisted. The Mediterranean was riddled with it.

Since there was nothing else to do she lay down on the bunk, but sleep evaded her. The boat was running smoothly under full sail, the water rippling along her sides, with an undulating movement when she breasted the swell. Now and again a larger wave would cause her to dip and rise. As she was a good sailor, the movement did not distress her, but she wished that she could be out on deck and not shut in the stuffy little cabin. Kneeling up on the bunk, she peered out of the porthole, but it was not far above deck level and all she could see was the strip of deck below it, and the rail beyond, bisecting an expanse of sky, in which a few stars showed, faded by the moon to specks of gilt. When the ship rolled, the dark wast of water through which she was travelling rose up to meet her vision.

She could hear the men moving about, and the murmur of their voices, Bruno's thick guttural accents, Mario's sharp incisive orders and Guido's laughter.

Then someone, she thought it must be Guido, climbed on to the cabin roof. He had some sort of stringed instrument, it sounded like a guitar, and he began to sing in a fruity tenor a very sentimental love song. Lorena suspected that it was being sung for her benefit, and it did dispel her suspicions. There could be nothing sinister about the crew's mission if he could sing so light-heartedly. She had to restrain an impulse to rap on the cabin ceiling in acknowledgement of this serenade. Mario had emphasised that he did not want Bruno to know of her presence and since she had invited herself aboard, it behoved her to respect his wishes.

That led her to speculate about the homeward journey. Presumably time was important, since Mario could not make a detour to put her ashore; the other two must have some sort of assignment to keep. They would be disembarked at some unknown port, and then Mario would set sail for home and she would be alone with him.

Recalling his dark presence, his hands upon her hair, she knew that he desired her, she was not so naïve that she did not realise that, and she would be helpless at his discretion. That lean muscular strength could easily overpower her and since he considered her to be a light woman, he would have no scruples about bending her to his will.

Misgivings assailed her, for he presented an even worse threat than Giulio, because she was unsure of her own reaction. It had been positive with regard to Giulio, the man revolted her, but Mario did not. Even at the thought of what might occur, a faint excitement stirred in her, an excitement of which she was ashamed, for she was not a girl who deliberately sought sensation, though unfortunately Mario might imagine that she was.

A curt command from the skipper cut short Guido's singing. She heard his laughing retort and the thud of his feet as he dropped to the deck. But though he had been silenced, the amorous notes still seemed to haunt the small cabin with a subtle message, which quickened Lorena's pulses.

Resolutely she changed the direction of her thoughts, recalling with relief the high esteem in which the Riccis held the boat's skipper. He was a man of integrity who seemed to be respected by his countrymen. She was allowing her imagination, stimulated by Guido's music to run away with her. Besides, if Mario were single-handed, the sailing of the boat would require all his attention. All that would happen would be an uneventful journey back and a formal parting on some landing stage, which she hoped would be near where she was staying. Once back in the villa, she would collect her gear and depart for a hotel. She remembered that it would be the day for which she had booked the car, and she could follow her original plan of exploring the interior. It was absurd to anticipate any romantic developments between the grim skipper and herself.

Peering out of the porthole, she saw what appeared to be a cloud looming on the horizon, but as the ship neared it, she saw lights above the cliff top and realised that it was another island. The boat glided in between perpendicular crags which cut off the moonlight. There were running footsteps overhead, the rattle of a sail being lowered. A bump alongside suggesting the presence of a rowing boat. There was a mutter of voices, and then clear above them, Guido's ringing tones:

'*Addio*, Mario, don't let the siren's charms distract you from your navigation, or you may be wrecked, in all senses.' He spoke in English so Bruno would not understand.

Mario's response was not distinguishable above the splash of oars as the dinghy shoved off, but clear over the water came a repeat of Guido's love-song. Evidently he was fully alive to the possibilities of the situation, and Lorena was relieved that it was the elder brother with whom she would have to contend.

The engine started up as the vessel was manoeuvred out of the cove. It turned about so suddenly that Lorena was thrown off the bunk. Picking herself up ruefully, she heard the engine splutter and die as the breeze caught the sails.

The return journey had begun, and the boat was presumably heading back to Sardinia, and surely Mario would not have misled her about that.

The words of a very old song came unbidden into her mind, though she had no recollection of where she had heard it.

'Once aboard the lugger and the girl is mine.'

A stupid song, with no bearing upon the present situation, she insisted to herself, but the words kept reiterating through her brain.

Moonlight flooded the little cabin as the boat drew away from the shadow of the cliffs, and she welcomed it gladly, the rocky coast had been forbidding. Occasional clouds flitted across the moon, but the boat ran smoothly through an oily sea under full sail.

By now Lorena was heartily sick of the confines of her prison, and judging by the time it had taken them to arrive at their destination, it would be some hours before she could disembark. Surely now she could go up on deck? She tried the door, but it was firmly fastened, the other door she knew only led into the fo'c'sle, which would be battened down.

Then she heard a footfall on the companionway, the bolt rattled, and the hatch slid open. Lorena retreated to the bunk, as Mario's torch flashed over her.

'Not asleep?' he asked.

'I don't find my present position inducive to slumber,' she said tartly. 'Where was that place?'

'Corsica.'

He was a menacing shadow looming over her in the small space of the cabin, but she welcomed his presence after her long solitude.

She said bluntly: 'Are you smuggling?'

'I told you I was not,' he returned.

'Then why is this whole expedition shrouded in mystery?'

'Ah, you are intrigued? Possibly you are imagining I belong to the Mafia or some such gang? But I am afraid the explanation is far less dramatic. Unfortunately I cannot satisfy your curiosity, as the family honour is involved.'

Piqued, she said loftily: 'I don't want to know your secrets. I'm only interested in your adventures insofar as they concern myself.'

'Your part in them will soon be over. We should make our landfall at sunrise. Would you like some coffee?'

'I'd love some. Can you make it in this rabbit hutch?'

'I could cook a dinner, but it is all ready in a thermos.'

He went to the galley and poured out a mugful of that beverage, which he handed to her. She drank it eagerly, aware that he was watching her, she could feel his gaze though she could not see his face. The moonlight washed over her, but it did not reach to illuminate his dark shape.

'Can't we have some light?' she asked.

'Why? You look charming silvered by the moon.'

'More than you do. What I can see of you looks sinister.'

He took the empty mug from her and then to her consternation sat down beside her on the bunk. He was so close, she could feel the rough wool of his sweater against her arm, and she was painfully conscious of his strong physical magnetism.

'Your brother got ashore all right?' she asked, trying to speak casually.

'He did; he is making for Ajaccio and Bruno will see him on his way.'

'Then ... then if we're alone, is the ship sailing herself?'

'More or less. She is on course and I have lashed the tiller, so unless the wind changes, I can keep you company.'

'Very considerate of you, but I hope you're going to be pleasant. I don't appreciate your snide thrusts at me.'

'I've paid you some compliments.'

'Backhanded ones.' She cast about in her mind for a safe

topic of conversation. 'Do you think the Riccis will make enquiries about me?' she asked, for it would be very reprehensible if they did not.

'Not until the morning, when you will be able to reassure them yourself. They must be quite used to lady guests becoming mislaid for the night.'

'Oh, you're abominable!' she cried fiercely. 'Every sentence you utter is an insinuation and an insulting one!'

'Calm down,' he advised. 'We still have a lot of time to kill, and it is a waste to spend it in vituperation.'

'Then please don't provoke me.'

'I will try not to do so,' he said with pretended meekness, but even in the faint light she could see the glint in his luminous eyes, cats' eyes, leopards' eyes—she wondered vaguely if he could see in the dark.

'By the way, what is your name?' he went on in a conversational tone. 'Laura? Lorna . . .?'

'Lorena.'

'*Si*, Lorena. A pretty name.'

She liked the way he said it, drawing out the middle syllable.

'So they thought in the fashion world,' she told him.

'Where you display yourself so shamelessly? I must admit you have something to display.'

Instinctively she hugged the robe closer to her body, although all he could see of her in the dimness was the moonlight silvering her hair.

'Where are you going to land me?' she asked, thinking the memory of this strange night would be as unsubstantial as a dream when it was over.

'Arachenza is the nearest anchorage.'

The prospect of being dumped on the quay in the chill of early morning in her bikini was not inviting. She said anxiously:

'Would you be so kind as to lend me this robe? I . . . I'll get it back to you somehow.'

62

'*Dio*, do you take me for a brute?' he asked reproachfully. 'I will find you something warmer than that, and hire a car to take you to the villa.' Remembering that she had told him she did not want to go back to it, he went on: 'You will have to return, you know, to collect your possessions.'

'Yes, yes, I know that.'

'And this time our parting will be final, Lorena.' He spoke with unnecessary emphasis, she thought, but he must have found her a great nuisance.

Unconsciously she sighed. 'Have I been very tiresome?'

'I would not say that. Your company is relieving the tedium of a solitary voyage.'

The mocking note had crept back into his voice and she edged away from him.

'I'm very grateful your ... er ... help,' she told him hesitantly, for he had not been very gracious in his manner of bestowing it, but he was bringing her back unharmed, and for that she was grateful.

He moved beside her, she could feel his muscular thigh against her leg, and her breathing quickened with the rapidity of her heartbeats. She was afraid he would notice it.

'There is a traditional way of expressing gratitude,' he suggested slyly.

Lorena shrank at the implication; she had been optimistic to think he would let her go without some demonstration. Kisses were common currency in modern society. Boys expected them after an evening's entertainment, and she had given them casually, with no more emotion behind them than a handshake, but the idea of kissing Mario threw her into a welter of agitation.

'Surely you're too adult to want to indulge in such a cheap exchange?' she said sharply.

He drew a quick intake of breath, and being so close to him, she could sense the tension in his body, the flexing of his muscles, as a leopard gathers itself together before it springs.

'So your kisses are cheap, Lorena?' he drawled. 'I rather thought as much. I wager Giulio does not have to ask for them.' His arm slid round her waist. 'Am I not entitled to my share of them?'

'No, please, Mario,' she cried desperately, trying with both her hands to dislodge his arm which enclosed her like a steel trap. 'It wouldn't be the same ... with you.'

'Why not?' He sounded amused. He was enjoying himself by playing with her, but he meant to have his way in the end.

'Because ... because. . . .' How could she explain that she could not take his advances lightly? He stirred her too profoundly, and she was afraid of what her response would be.

'I am a man, am I not?' he asked silkily. 'You do not find me repugnant?'

With a flash of spirit, she retorted: 'I find your present conduct so.'

'Rubbish,' he exclaimed. 'You like it. I am not made of ice, nor are you. What are you afraid of? No one will know, and the situation is fortuitous.'

She had run from Giulio with revulsion, but Mario did not revolt her, that was what made her present predicament so humiliating. She knew that if he had had any respect for her, he would not treat her so, and he had the effrontery to suppose that she wanted his advances.

His arm, gripping her waist, drew her closer, and with all her strength she tried to fend him off, while she gasped:

'I didn't think you would be such a heel as to take advantage of my helplessness. I ... I believed you were chivalrous.'

'Chivalrous? That's an odd word to hear from one of your set, which doesn't know the meaning of the word. Is not this what you have been anticipating all night? I would hate to disappoint you. This is what your sort expects from a man.'

Her puny resistance was completely ineffective. She had been kissed and embraced before, she could not have reached her twenty-two years in a permissive age without experimenting, but her experiences had always left her cold. Mario overwhelmed her. Her face, her throat, and finally her mouth were ravaged, while the arms that held her crushed like a vice, but she was far from feeling outraged. Some primitive urge, long buried beneath her sophisticated veneer, rose up and submerged her. She met his flame with fire. Her arms instinctively went around his neck, her lips parted under his, her body became fluid in his grasp. She was oblivious to the quite considerable pain which he was inflicting upon her.

Then the ship began to rock violently.

Instantly Mario flung her from him and leaped to his feet, his nautical instincts overriding his desire.

'A sudden squall,' he said tersely. 'I should have kept a better watch, but with such a diversion....' He grinned wickedly. 'Stay where you are, you are in no danger.'

He clambered through the hatch, and Lorena could hear the canvas flapping above their heads. The boat heeled over alarmingly, so that Lorena slid to the floor.

She scrambled up, breathless and bewildered, shocked by the violence of her own reactions. She had never imagined that any man could rouse her as this smuggler, pirate or whatever he was, had done. That there was a physical attraction between them had been apparent almost from the first, but she knew such lures were a trap, which had caught less sophisticated girls in an entanglement they had come to regret bitterly. She was furious with herself for yielding to it. Mario had a bad enough opinion of her without adding to it by easy surrender. He had said that what he had done was what she expected from a man, and her reaction had proved him right. He was insufferable, she thought wildly, beating with her clenched fist on the padding of the bunk; he had taken advantage of her helplessness, and heaven knew what he would do next. The mere thought of the various possibilities caused her pulses to race.

She became aware that the boat was pitching and rolling ominously, and the cabin was as dark as the inside of a tomb, except for occasional flashes of lightning.

As the storm within her abated, she became fully conscious of the elemental storm raging about the ship. It had come up very quickly as storms sometimes did in those waters and Mario had been too occupied with her to notice its approach. Sudden panic gripped her. The confined space of the cabin made her feel like a rat in a trap. If she were going to be drowned, she would rather be drowned in the open.

She stumbled towards the hatchway, while the cabin floor rose and fell beneath her feet. She peered out up into the cockpit. A flicker of lightning showed her Mario at the tiller, his face raised to the sky. Rain was lashing down upon the deck. Rigging creaked above her head. Mario had hove to, and the boat was stoutly riding out the storm, but Lorena was no mariner, to know that; she was terrified as the tossing waves rose first on one side and then the other, and spray and spume flew over the deck. She was convinced the ship was in imminent danger of being swamped.

Wanting the comfort of another human presence, she clambered out of shelter, making for the cockpit and was instantly soaked, her hair flew out like a banner in the wind, but she did not heed her condition, she was intent only upon reaching Mario.

It was not so dark outside as in the cabin and the light illuminating the compass shone up into Mario's face. The rain streamed from his hair, he had peeled off his soaking jersey and was naked to the waist, and far from being dismayed by their predicament, he wore an expression of savage exultation. He was actually enjoying the fury of the elements—a wild man warring with the storm.

'Mario!' Lorena gasped, scrambling up the steps to the cockpit and clutching at the surrounding coaming. 'Mario, are we going down?'

He could not hear her, close as she was, for the tumult of the weather, but he saw her.

'Get below!' he shouted. 'There is no danger.'

Dense masses of cloud were racing overhead, but a line of light in the east showed that the storm was passing.

Mario shouted to her again to get below. Reluctantly she turned round, shivering with cold as the realisation of her soaked robe penetrated her consciousness. She slipped, her numbed fingers grasping at the air, and fell into a dark pit of nothingness.

CHAPTER FOUR

OF the period which followed, Lorena never recollected more than vague impressions, only one of which was strong and indelible. There was a dark-faced woman, who gave her drugs which sent her back into uneasy oblivion, but she was only a shadow, it was the other presence which reached her consciousness even during her delirium. It had hands, strong yet gentle, which held her, stilling her with tender insistence until she became quiet, but she had no idea of its identity. She was reminded of her father, who so often had soothed her childish woes, and such was her confusion, she thought vaguely it must be he.

Once she grasped words which were intelligible, something about her hair. It hung heavy and tangled about her shoulders and she murmured: 'So hot ... so hot.'

'It must be cut off,' said liquid Italian syllables.

This pronouncement met with a vigorous denial.

Someone drew a comb through its meshes, patiently disentangling every knot and snarl, braiding it neatly, but in her frenzy, she soon tore it loose again, to have the process repeated, but however restless she was, the combing always quieted her.

She did not know where she was or who was tending her, whether it was day or night; she was only aware of the hands combing her hair.

Then one morning she awoke from deep sleep to find her fever had left her, and although pitifully weak, she had regained her senses.

She discovered that she was lying on a high iron bedstead in a little room with a bare wooden floor and no curtains at the square of window through which the sun was pouring. A small table beside the bed held a pottery jug filled with fresh lemonade and a mug. In one corner was a primitive washstand with a crude toilet set in earthenware. The furnishings were completed by a couple of wooden chairs and a carved crucifix hanging upon one wall.

Where was she and what had happened? The last thing that she remembered was the storm at sea, which obviously she had survived. She then discovered that she was wearing a coarse linen nightdress and her hair was in two plaits on either side of her brow—so it had not been cut off, but who had dressed it? Knitting her brows, she fingered it. Why had she thought that someone had wanted to cut it off? She must have been very ill, and her recollections were only figments of her sick imagination, certainly her father could not have been there. She was too weak and exhausted to ponder further and she dozed.

Some time later the creak of the door brought her fully awake. The girl who entered was short and small-boned like most of the Sards, but she held herself so proudly, walking with the free carriage of those who for generations had carried their burdens upon their heads, that she appeared much taller than she was. Her big dark eyes were direct and questioning, but surprisingly she was wearing a dark mini-skirt and a red jumper, while her rich black hair was cut short. Her costume was so modern that Lorena blinked, it did not fit in with the primitive appearance of the room.

'You are awake, *signorina*?' the girl asked in Italian.

Lorena smiled and tried to sit up, but she fell back against the coarse linen of her pillow.

'Oh, but I'm weak!' she exclaimed in English.

The girl came swiftly towards her, and laid her hand upon her forehead, while her other hand sought for her pulse.

'You must expect to be so,' she said in the same tongue. 'You have been most ill, but the fever he has gone.'

'You speak English?' Lorena was surprised.

'*Si, signorina*. I train to be nurse in Italy and I learn to

69

speak it in Rome. When my grandmother ill, I come back to look after her. Now she is better I think to go home, so it was fortunate that I was still here to nurse you.'

'That was very kind of you,' Lorena told her gratefully, 'but where am I?'

The girl named the village, and Lorena was startled, for she had read about it. It bore a sinister sound, for it was here, some ten years ago, that an ill-fated New Zealand couple had been shot, having apparently walked into the middle of a vendetta. The matter had never been wholly cleared up. The body of a Sard was afterwards found in the same spot, and seemed to indicate that vengeance had been taken upon the man who had shot them, but why he had done so was never to be known. Since then there had been occasional incidents, for the village was situated in wild, remote country, but for all that, excursions were now being run to it.

'But how on earth did I get here?' she asked.

'Signor Marescu bring you. This is the house of his grandmother, who is my grandmother also. I am called Assunta Corrias.'

Lorena looked round the primitive little room which contrasted pitifully with her quarters at the Riccis' villa. Had Mario brought her here to show her the reverse side of Sardo life, the tough, rough existence which he had mentioned on the plane? Did he think that such an experience would be salutary for her? But why bring her here at all; surely it would have been more sensible to return her to her friends instead of inflicting her upon his relations?

She looked at Assunta with her eyes full of questions, and the Sardo girl said:

'You have been most ill and you must not trouble your brain. When you are stronger you may talk and I will tell you more. Now you must rest. What is your name?'

Lorena told her, surprised that Mario had not mentioned it. Perhaps he had been unable to remember it, or perhaps he did not want Assunta to know who she was. Her mind was still seething with questions, but Assunta, seeing stress in her face, insisted that she must be quiet, everything would be explained in good time, but now she must rest.

She went away to fetch the invalid some breakfast.

Left alone, Lorena reconstructed the events previous to her illness. Her last recollection was of falling down the companionway. She must have knocked herself out. She felt her head gingerly and found a tender spot which had been a bruise. She had been wet through, and that following the exposure she had suffered during her swim was enough to cause the fever which Assunta had mentioned, coupled with the turmoil of emotions which had assailed her, culminating in that wild scene in the cabin. What would have happened, she wondered, if the storm had not arisen? She went hot all over at the recollection. She, proud sophisticated Lorena Lawrence, who had extricated herself from more than one tricky situation in the course of her career, had nearly succumbed to a strange man, who by some accident of alchemy had roused in her a passion of which she had not known herself to be capable. She had been wax in his hands, ready to receive any imprint he wished to impress upon her. She ought to be bitterly ashamed, but she had gloried in it, and even in retrospect she could not regret what had happened, for in those hectic moments she had discovered her womanhood.

The perplexing question remained unanswered—why had he brought her here instead of dumping her in the nearest hospital? Could it be that he intended to complete what had been interrupted, and would she be strong enough to resist him? Was he living in this house? She looked again at its primitive furnishings; if he did, he seemed to exist in poor circumstances, yet he did not appear to be a poor man. His clothes were well tailored, he had driven away from the villa in an expensive private car, he was acclaimed by the Ricci set, who had no use for a pauper.

71

When Assunta returned with coffee and rolls, she asked her anxiously:

'Does Signor Marescu live here?'

Assunta laughed. 'Certainly not. He has his own house in Nuoro, which is far more splendid than this is.'

That information was a relief, but still more puzzling.

'Then why did he bring me here?'

'Because he know that I am competent nurse and can care for you.'

'But surely there are hospitals....'

'You ask too many questions, you put your temperature up again. Now you must sleep.'

Since she was very weak, Lorena abandoned her problems and was glad to obey her nurse.

Assunta continued to steadily refuse to answer any of Lorena's queries. She knew nothing about her cousin's motives, she insisted. Lorena must wait until he came and ask him herself, an occurrence which Lorena anticipated with some trepidation. She needed to feel a great deal stronger before she could cope with Mario.

In the evening, the grandmother came to visit her and to note her progress.

Lucia Marescu was tiny, with high flat cheekbones and almond-shaped eyes. Through the centuries the blood of many nationalities had mingled with the original inhabitants, but Lucia was a possible throwback to the original stock. She looked neither Italian, Arab nor Greek, though types of all three races could be found in the seaports. She was in fact *il vero Sard*, the true Sard. The opaque black eyes in the wrinkled brown face were guardians of ancient secrets, and she carried herself with pride. She wore a long pleated woollen shirt and a black shawl, the traditional daily wear of the island countrywomen.

To Lorena's astonishment, she addressed her in English with an American accent, and noticing the girl's surprised look, as she greeted her formally, she proceeded to explain.

'I learned it from my daughter-in-law—she was half American. My son met her when he was doing his military service in Italy when she was on holiday there. It was a marriage in haste, to be greatly regretted.' She sighed. 'Jane could not stick life on the island. She pined for Broadway and the city lights, and she went back to the States. She was a tall woman, that is why Mario is a big man.'

Lorena reflected that the foreign mother explained more about Mario than his height. She sensed that he resented the alien blood in him, and his advocacy of the simple life was engendered by a passionate desire to identify himself with his countrymen. He resented her and her associates at the villa because they were foreigners.

'Is your son still alive?' she asked.

Lucia sighed again. 'He die much too young in an accident. Mario and Guido have no one but me to bring them up. It is a bad thing. Boys need a man to keep them out of mischief.'

Lorena wondered what mischief the pair had been up to on the night when she had invaded their boat, but she had better not speak of that to Lucia.

'I'm afraid I've been a great imposition upon your kindness,' she said apologetically, 'but it wasn't my doing. Now I'm better I must see about getting home.'

She would like to be gone before Mario came, but it might be difficult to do so without his help. The house party would have disbanded, but what had happened to her belongings, her travellers' cheques and passport? Without them she was stranded. Did her friends know what had become of her?

Signora Marescu gave her a sharp look.

'You aren't fit to travel. You must stay here for the present.'

'Thank you,' Lorena murmured, 'but. . . .'

'It's better for all concerned that you stay here,' Lucia

73

insisted so emphatically that Lorena glanced at her dubiously.

'There's so much I don't understand,' she complained, knitting her brows. 'Why I was brought to you at all.' She wondered what story Mario had concocted to account for her appearance.

'You delirious, you rave,' the old woman told her. 'You mutter very odd things about both my grandsons, which you would not wish strangers to hear any more than Mario did.'

Lorena wondered what on earth she had said.

'Nobody takes any notice of a sick person's ravings,' she said impatiently. 'If I were so ill, I might have died.'

'You had the best of care here,' Lucia assured her. 'Assunta is very efficient nurse.'

'Yes, of course.' But not the same scientific treatment she would have received in a hospital.

'I also have some skill with simples,' Lucia went on. 'I know how to make the medicine which soothes.'

Lorena looked at her askance. She did look like a little brown witch with her big nose and sharp chin. She remembered stories that she had heard about the primitive peasantry in the interior, where superstition was rife and witchcraft still held sway. It seemed incongruous alongside the sophistication of the Emerald Coast, but in this village she was back in an earlier age.

She saw the old woman's black eyes were studying her intently as if reading her thoughts.

'No fancy modern medicine could have done more for you than mine,' she assured her.

'I'm most grateful.' Lorena wondered what poisons had been administered to her, but anyhow they seemed to have effected a cure.

Lucia said deliberately:

'My grandson is most anxious for your full recovery, but he also insists that you do not leave here too soon. The mountain air is healthy and will give you back your strength. He has been called away on business, but he will in due course return. He could not take you to his own house, since he is a bachelor, but will not be one for much longer, I hope.'

There flashed back into Lorena's mind the conversation at dinner on her first night at the Riccis', when Giulio had mentioned that Mario was contracted to a 'black-browed gypsy'. She had forgotten the allusion until now, and she recalled it with a curious sinking of her heart.

'Yes, I did hear he was engaged,' she murmured.

'From his infancy. Margherita Segni is a very sweet girl,' Lucia said with satisfaction. 'Not only will she have a fine dowry, but she is a true Sard.' The black eyes fixed themselves significantly upon Lorena's face. 'It is not well to marry outside one's country. I have told you how it was with my son. The fair hair, the white skin appeal to the dark men of the South, but they are too fiery for the cool daughters of the north. The fires burn away and nothing is left but discontent. Mario understands this very well, he will only marry one of his own people.'

Lorena knew this speech was intended to convey a warning, and she again wondered uneasily what she had said in her delirium. Mario had certainly been fiery in the cabin, but her own response had not been cool, in fact it had been shameful. She was thankful Lucia did not know about that. She said a little stiffly:

'If you're thinking of me, I've no intention of marrying anyone, and I wish Signor Marescu happiness with his bride.'

Lucia sighed for a third time. 'The young are so headstrong,' she complained. 'They do not know what is best. Assunta's mother, she would not marry the man chosen for her, and now she must live in Italy where her husband works, and can rarely visit her home.'

'But if she loved him. . . .' Lorena began.

Lucia made a gesture of contempt. 'Love is a marshlight, a delusion, it doesn't last,' she declared. 'It is the solid things that are more important, position, shared interests, compatibility. *Grazie a dio*, Mario will never be so foolish as to be led astray by love. He is old enough to know how ephemeral it is.'

More warnings, Lorena wondered, but she could not imagine Mario in love. Love surely meant tenderness, consideration, even reverence, but all he could feel was desire.

Then Assunta came in and insisted that she must rest.

'Mario will be angry with me if you have the relapse,' she said.

'I don't think he'd worry,' Lorena announced a little bitterly, for as far as she knew, Mario had not enquired about her since she had been in the village.

The two women exchanged glances.

'He make me responsible,' Assunta declared stolidly. 'Please repose yourself, *signorina*.'

Reluctantly Lorena obeyed.

Being young and healthy, Lorena improved rapidly and was soon able to sit in the walled garden behind the house. Though the latter presented an uncompromising stone front to the road, it had, like many Sardo houses, a garden behind it enclosed by high walls. The small space was full of flowers and bushes, jasmine and clematis festooning the house, oleanders, carnations, lilies, thyme and lavender perfuming the air. Here for the first time Lorena heard the clicking of the cicadas, and here she made the acquaintance of Gigi, in fact he became her constant companion, seeming fascinated by her, to him, unusual appearance.

For Assunta, it transpired, was a widow, and Gigi—his full name was Giovanni after his father—was her five-year-old son. She had married at what seemed to Lorena the ridiculous age of sixteen, but Latin girls mature young. Her husband had perished in a storm at sea.

'We are not lucky with our men,' Assunta had said with a

sad little smile. 'La Nonna lose her son, my uncle, and I my husband. Only Mario and Guido are left.'

It was because she was widowed that Assunta had taken up nursing, finding in hard work and tending others relief for her own heartache. Normally she lived with her parents, who had no other children, but she, as she had said, had come to Sardinia to nurse Lucia when she had needed her.

'And I bring Gigi too. The island nice change for him,' she had explained.

He had mischievous brown eyes in a puckish face and was delighted to find someone who had leisure to give him undivided attention and he did much to relieve the tedium of Lorena's convalescence. She amused them both by filling in the gaps in his English, though he told her candidly his language was much prettier than hers.

So she whiled away the sunny hours sitting in the open air, while she recovered her strength, playing with Gigi and listening to Assunta's confidences. The Sardo girl, unlike her grandmother, wholeheartedly believed in love.

'It is the most wonderful thing in life,' she declared fervently, her dark eyes glowing. 'I had four perfect years with my Giovanni, they crown my life.'

'You're still very young,' Lorena said gently. 'Couldn't there be another love?'

'Perhaps, but it would be different,' Assunta stated. She looked at Lorena curiously. 'But you, *signorina*, have you not loved?'

She was astonished when Lorena admitted that she had not.

Assunta was insatiably curious about the Riccis, for she knew Lorena had been staying with them. To please her, Lorena described the villa and the owners' way of life, and she listened as if to a fairy tale. To Lorena too it all seemed unreal and remote; the simple life she was leading now was so much more genuine. Assunta's means were apparently very modest.

77

'Of course Mario always ready to help, he is not poor,' she told Lorena, 'but . . .' she lifted her head proudly, 'we do not accept charity from him.'

'But after all, he's a near relation,' Lorena pointed out.

'That is no reason to—what you say—sponge on him,' Assunta insisted. 'But he offer to educate Gigi, and that I shall not refuse. Except himself, Gigi is the only male in the family, until Mario marry.'

'What about Guido?' Lorena asked.

'He go to his mother's people, he become Americano,' Assunta said disdainfully. 'He not come back.'

She refused to say anything more about her younger cousin, and Lorena was left with the impression that Guido had been exiled in disgrace, and what she had heard on the boat seemed to confirm it.

She became anxious about her parents, who would be wondering at her prolonged absence, and Assunta's assertion that Mario would have done what was necessary to reassure them about her safety was not convincing. There was no reason from his point of view why he should do anything of the sort. Her tentative suggestion that she might send them a postcard met with a stern veto, and being penniless, she had not the money for a stamp. In this connection Lucia told her:

'You must trust us, *signorina*. We have done our best for you and you owe us some gratitude for our care. But without Mario's approval I cannot allow you to send messages, and you can be sure no one in the village will abet you.'

The expression on her wrinkled face was almost threatening.

'Then I'm virtually a prisoner?' Lorena asked bluntly.

'An honoured guest,' Lucia corrected her. 'We share with you all that we have. You came to us with nothing.'

Lorena was wearing an old skirt and blouse belonging to Assunta and she felt rebuked.

'Mario will come as soon as he can,' Lucia went on.

78

'When he will, no doubt, arrange for your journey home. In the meantime you must be patient, *signorina*.'

To be expected to wait patiently until Mario conde-scended to remember her offended Lorena's independent spirit. She would prefer not to encounter him again, but though the village possessed both a bank and a post office they had no doubt been warned not to help her, since the Marescus seemed to govern the place. But there were other towns and villages, where she could find aid, if she con-cocted a convincing story to account for being stranded. She only had to walk until she found one.

However, she was forced to realise that that idea was quite impracticable, when, accompanied by Assunta and Gigi, she was able to walk a little way up the side of the mountain above the village, which lay in a narrow band below its crest.

The place had been built in a strategic position with all the approaches clearly visible for miles around, while the road leading up to it was steep and winding. The valleys in Sardinia are not deep ravines like those among the Alps, but are wide and rolling, between green mountains heavily wooded, with expanses of *macchia*, the scrub composed of cistus, myrtle and small evergreen oaks, which is equivalent to the Corsican *maquis*.

Looking over the spread of sparsely populated forest and upland, she could see that she was completely cut off from civilisation and she would have to walk for many miles before she encountered a soul.

Gigi ran about waving a shepherd's crook, herding an imaginary flock of sheep, shouting:

'I'se Aurelio—I'se Aurelio!'

He was fascinated by the *pastori*—the shepherds—As-sunta explained, men who roamed the uplands with the sheep, for though pigs and cattle grazed at large, the sheep were herded, the ewes' milk being used for cheese.

'Aurelio is a shepherd,' Assunta informed her, 'and Gigi

79

is friendly with him. In the summertime the *pastori* live with the sheep. They have huts for shelter, most primitive. Gigi want very much to go to Aurelio's hut, but it is too far for little legs.'

Feeling that Assunta was more sympathetic than her grandmother, Lorena took this opportunity while she was alone with her to mention her desire to be gone and at once.

'But, *signorina*, you must have money and a passport,' the girl pointed out.

'Don't I know it!' Lorena cried. 'But I've got both, and if I could contact my friends I could find out where they are, or ask them to get in touch with my family.'

'Mario say your friends not nice people,' Assunta announced smugly.

Exasperated, Lorena exclaimed rashly: 'He needn't be so pi about them, considering the way he goes on himself.'

Assunta looked at her reproachfully out of velvet brown eyes.

'I do not know what means "go on",' she said. 'Mario a good man. He say you stay here till he come, and he will come soon.'

'So you keep telling me, but he delays and delays. I'm quite all right now, and I won't say anything about that boat trip, so why can't I go?'

Assunta looked uneasy, casting a cautious glance behind her, then she said warningly:

'*Signorina*, I do not know how you come to be on Mario's boat, I do not seek to know, though I think Margherita Segni would be interested.' Lorena started. She was always forgetting Mario's fiancée. 'It is enough that he ask my help. Here we all have our secrets, and we do not enquire into the secrets of others. There is much that is hidden and wisely so. Please be patient, Mario will come.'

Lorena found this cryptic speech extremely irritating. She saw no necessity for cloak-and-dagger mysteries, but

Assunta had all the Latin love of intrigue.

'Suppose I don't want to see him?' she asked rebelliously.

Assunta smiled knowingly. 'I think you do.'

A hot denial rose to Lorena's lips, but at that moment Gigi came up behind her, and putting his crook round her throat, pulled her over backwards.

'Got you!' he yelled triumphantly.

Assunta scolded him vigorously, for he might have hurt their visitor, while Lorena picked herself up, declaring she was all right. The subject of Mario was dropped. She was disappointed by Assunta's non-co-operation, and the mention of Margherita had caused her to suspect that Mario's real reason for sequestering her in the village was that he feared his betrothed might have come to learn of their midnight adventure. If she had been taken to hospital, an inquisitive pressman might have wormed out the story, and apparently the Sards were sticklers for the conventions. But her conjectures led nowhere, and it seemed that she had no option but to await Mario's coming and she hoped that would not be delayed much longer. He had treated her with scant consideration, going off into the blue, leaving her stranded, and he had not even bothered to ascertain if she had recovered before he left.

Assunta was right about one thing, she thought with a certain wry amusement; no fiancée would appreciate what had passed between Mario and herself in his cabin. The Sardo girl had a problem if that were his usual conduct with his female acquaintances when he got them alone.

But even if she were a foreigner, and a girl he did not think he need respect, surely he owed Margherita some fidelity? Perhaps if it were an arranged marriage, as seemed probable, he saw no harm in indulging his fancies before assuming the yoke of matrimony.

But this fancy isn't going to be caught again, she assured herself firmly. When Signor Mario Marescu does condescend to turn up, I shall have a lot to say to him and it won't be complimentary.

A strong breeze was blowing on the day when Mario eventually appeared. Lorena was taking a stroll down the main street, which wound between tall, grey stone houses, brightened by gaily painted doors and window frames. Dust and fallen leaves swirled along the cobbles and her spirits had sunk to zero.

The big black car approached her from the opposite direction, nosing along the narrow road and its driver, perceiving her, drew up. She recognised Mario with a lurch of her heart.

He was wearing a grey suit and looked very different from his appearance on the boat, very civilised and formal. As he sprang out to greet her, she noticed anew how much taller and slimmer he was than the majority of his short stocky countrymen. The American mother, she thought, but there was nothing American about the fathomless eyes in his brown falcon's face and the imperial carriage of his head. They were a heritage from a much older stock.

'Lorena, it is good to see you well again,' he exclaimed with his brilliant smile.

She became painfully conscious of her own appearance. Her hair had been ruffled by the wind, her white short-sleeved blouse was no longer fresh, her shapeless shirt, which belonged to Assunta's pre-mini period, flapped against her bare legs, while her feet were encased in espadrilles. It was he who had reduced her to such straits and her heart swelled with indignation.

'*Buon giorno*, Signor Marescu,' she said coldly.

He raised his eyebrows ironically. 'How very formal! I thought we had broken down the barriers before the storm broke.'

She clenched her hands. 'Oh, you ... you're shameless!' she gasped.

'So were you,' he returned amiably, adding as she turned

away, 'Pax, *signorina*, let us forget that episode ever happened. I have much to say to you. Please to get into the car, and I will drive you out into the country where we can talk without interruption.'

She hesitated, and he said impatiently:

'*Va bene*, there will be no frolics today. I have come to arrange about your departure.'

He opened the door on the passenger side and her grey eyes sparkled resentfully as she slipped inside.

'I've plenty to say to you,' she announced. 'You've got a lot of explaining to do, Signor Marescu.'

'I have, have I?'

He got in beside her and turned the car about. In spite of her ruffled feelings, Lorena found she was ridiculously glad to see him. He was a link with civilisation, and she was heartily sick of the primitive limitations of the village.

The car slithered down the rough, winding track that led away from the village in tortuous bends. Reaching an intersection, Mario turned westwards and drove for some while in silence, and Lorena looked about her with interest.

There were patches of dry *macchia*, terraced vineyards and groves of cork trees. Outside one village, a small *nuraghe* stood on an eminence, one of the truncated unmortared stone towers from prehistoric times, which were so much a feature of the island.

'There are much finer specimens in the south and west,' Mario told her, 'some large enough to accommodate several hundred people, with a well in the centre. They must have been quite impregnable against the weapons in use in those days.'

But Lorena was in no mood for a lecture on the island's history. She said sharply:

'How much farther have we to go before you're going to explain yourself?'

'I want to show you a view which I think you will appreciate,' he returned mildly. 'A beautiful setting might make you feel more charitably disposed towards me.'

'It'll need to be something quite extraordinary to do that.'

He had turned south and the road climbed upwards in steep hairpin bends. There was a dense and lovely fringe to it of flowers; poppies, honeysuckle, scabious and vetch among others, while blackberry blossom in clusters rose above this wild herbaceous border. There was also thyme and rosemary to add fragrance to the air, and sweet chestnut trees smothered in creamy yellow blossom among the oaks, while above it all was a blue, blue sky, across which billowy white clouds raced like galleons in full sail.

As the road climbed even higher, southwards and slightly to the east, the tops of the more lofty mountains appeared above the uplands and Lorena forgot her indignation, even her companion's presence, in the grandeur of the scene. Then at last Mario halted the car. He pointed to the distant purple line of mountains.

'That is the edge of the Gennargentu, the Silver Gate, so called because in winter the sun turns its snows to argent.'

Lorena stared awestruck at the layers upon layers of mountains receding into the distance, most of which were thickly wooded. Although they lacked the magnificence of the Alps, they were fine, rolling heights, covering acres of wild country.

The air was cool with a wonderful freshness, and she wound down her window to let the breeze, the wind had dropped, blow on her face. Birds were singing, butterflies had settled like delicate mosaics on the myriad blooms, favouring the purple flowering thistles.

Mario said: 'Those forests are full of game, wild boar and deer. Also foxes, martens, even wild cats and a few of the fabled *muffloni*, the rare mountain sheep.'

'Does anybody live there?' she asked.

'Charcoal burners and the *banditti*. They lack for nothing, having meat, fresh water and fuel on the doorstep, so to speak.'

At the mention of bandits, the scene became slightly sinister and she shivered involuntarily. It was a lonely spot and it was not difficult to imagine desperate men lurking behind the trees.

'The men who have killed in a vendetta?' she enquired, remembering what he had said about that.

'Some of them.' He was looking sombre. 'They have the perfect hideout in there. This is a place of fierce loyalties, sudden violence and many secrets, and one thing is certain, no Sard will ever betray his neighbour. The *carabinieri*'s questions are met with the *omerta*—silence.'

The magnificence of the scenery had momentarily driven her own grievances from her mind, but now she recalled them, and turning her shoulder to the mountains and the flowers, she faced her companion.

'Now perhaps you'll break your personal silence and answer a few questions. I want to know why I was brought to your grandmother's house instead of being taken to a hospital, and why I'm not allowed to communicate with my friends; also what's happened to my belongings, and whether anybody knows where I am, and ... well, what's it all about?'

'What an inquisition!' he remarked coolly. He leaned back negligently in his seat, his black eyes regarding her through half closed lids. 'Dealing with the first one, my grandmother and Assunta were perfectly capable of nursing you. Hospital you might have found very expensive. You were badly concussed from falling on your head and you developed a chill and then fever. Why you could not stay in the cabin I cannot conceive. The damage was entirely your own fault.'

'So you blame me for everything?' she asked angrily.

'I do. I didn't ask you to come aboard my boat. Your presence was something I could have very well done without.'

85

'In spite of the amusement I provided for you?' she asked scathingly, and a flicker of—could it be shame?—crossed his face.

'That too I would have been better without.'

Lorena turned her gaze to the cloud shadows passing over the uplands. She had to admit his accusation was not entirely unfair, but that did not lessen her resentment.

'Weren't there any enquiries made for me?' she asked, for she was unable to believe that the Ricci party could have taken her disappearance with complete indifference.

'Apparently your delightful friend Giulio told them that when he went to bring you off, he could not find you, and he concluded that either you had attempted to swim to the port and had been washed out to sea, or you had been picked up by some boat.'

She stared at him horrified. 'Have they told my parents I've been reported missing?' she cried. 'I must let them know at once that I'm still alive. If you have any decency at all, you'll help me to send a wire.'

'That will not be necessary.'

'It is! It is!' In her agitation she clutched his arm and felt his muscles tense under her hands.

'I mean it has already been covered,' he told her, gently detaching her clinging fingers. 'I contacted that red-haired woman, what is her name? Venetia something, and asked her send your family a card saying your return had been delayed. She also packed your things and I have them with me. I would have brought them before, but I had an urgent call to go to Genoa on business. I told her that you had been picked up unconscious and brought to my grandmother's house, but I'm rather afraid she imagined that we were enjoying an unofficial honeymoon together.' He smiled wickedly.

'I hope you undeceived her.'

'How could I, since she did not express her thought, but it was plain on her face. It is what she would think.'

'Oh!' Lorena put her hands before her eyes to shut out his mocking face. She was overcome with mortification. She knew that was just the interpretation Venetia would put upon the situation, nor would she keep her suspicions to herself, and how the men she had snubbed would triumph! Mario was obviously enjoying her embarrassment; he did not care about the slur upon her good name, because he believed it was already sullied. The Sards, like the Italians, guarded their women jealously and that mad moment of surrender in the cabin would have cheapened her still further in his eyes.

He was watching her closely with an inscrutable expression.

'However, your friend Giulio's comments were beyond a joke. I had to knock him down.'

'Ah!' She drew a long breath. 'I'm glad you did that.'

'Are you?' He seemed pleased. 'I gather, from what he let drop, that he was the monster who was coming to devour Andromeda when I did my Perseus act in spiriting you away.'

'Andromeda was chained to the rock through no fault of her own, and Perseus behaved like a gentleman.'

'Meaning I did not?' The black eyes were mocking again. 'I suit my manners to my company.'

'Indeed?' she said icily. Then, maddened by his cool detachment, she asked recklessly: 'Then are you keeping me here until you have another chance to seduce me?'

He froze into stern immobility. 'Certainly not. My grandmother's house is not the place for such capers,' he said haughtily.

She remembered again that he was engaged to a Sardo girl, Margherita, which made his past conduct all the more reprehensible, though now he seemed as anxious to obliterate that episode as she was.

'Then what are you keeping me for?' she asked angrily.

He said uncertainly: 'For one thing, you were off your

87

head.'

'So you and your brother were up to something shady,' she flashed.

His eyes flickered. 'So you've cast us both as a pair of villains?' he suggested. 'I do not know what strange would have made of your revelations. It was safer to keep you in the family.'

This observation was far from satisfying her. She stared at him resentfully, but he was unconcernedly searching his pockets for his cigarettes.

'Will you have one?' he asked politely, offering his case. He had become remote, his dark eyes hard as ebony, his face like carved granite. Impossible to credit that he was the same man as the one who had kissed her so passionately. Though he had been teasingly provocative, there was no hint today of the latent fires which she had glimpsed, and then she must be looking supremely unattractive in Assunta's cast-off clothes with her hair in a mess.

She accepted a cigarette, though she rarely smoked, but she felt the need of something to sustain her. Both his case and his lighter looked expensive. She wondered vaguely how he made his money, since Lucia seemed far from affluent. Nor did his well cut suit and careful grooming match up with her own shabby appearance.

'You might have brought my things before you went gallivanting off to Genoa,' she said reproachfully. 'I've had to go about in rags.'

'I see nothing ragged about you except perhaps your temper,' he retorted, 'and you are more decently clad than when I last saw you.'

She flushed and turned her head away, for then she had been near naked. Continuing to regard her satirically, he went on:

'The village would not have been impressed by your sophisticated glamour, little butterfly, its denizens might even have been shocked, and it will have done you no harm to live rough for a while.'

'I'm not a butterfly,' she denied hotly, 'I'm a working girl.'

He picked up one of her hands, looking critically at the white slender fingers, the delicate filbert nails.

'Hardly a worker's hand,' he drawled.

She snatched it away. 'I have to keep them nice for my job. There are other ways of working than with one's hands.'

'So you keep telling me, but our ideas upon that subject differ. When I first saw you, I thought you were the epitome of idle luxury the perfection of the beautician and the couturier's arts. Now I am seeing the real girl stripped of her trimmings, and....' He broke off and stubbed out his cigarette.

'You are disillusioned?' she suggested.

He gave her an odd smile but said nothing.

Wanting to penetrate his irritating self-possession, she said sweetly:

'You're engaged to be married, aren't you? Would your fiancée be pleased to hear that you've got a kept woman in the hills?'

He raised his eyebrows. 'What are you trying to do now? Blackmail me? For shame, Lorena!'

'Blackmailing is no worse than smuggling.'

'I've told you repeatedly I was not smuggling,' he said patiently.

'Then what's all the mystery about your brother?'

He looked at her consideringly. 'It really is not your business,' he rebuked her gently, 'but to save further misapprehensions, I will tell that I wanted to land Guido unobtrusively upon Corsica, from whence he will make his way to the States.' He paused, seemingly to pick his words. 'It was necessary that he should go away.'

'But why? Was he engaged upon one of your famous vendettas?'

A certain tenseness about his attitude told her she had hit upon the truth. 'Oh, no,' she cried. 'That's too fantastic in this day and age.'

'It might not have come to that,' he said quietly. 'The young idiot had become involved with a married woman. Ghisu had sworn to have his blood. He is a violent man and old-fashioned and believes it is up to him to avenge his honour. He is also a dead shot. Guido has always wanted to go to the States, where we have connections. So we arranged to go fishing one night, as we often do, and I returned alone. Satisfied?'

'Sounds like a bad thriller,' she said scornfully. 'All that secrecy. Why couldn't you just put him on a plane for America?'

'That would have looked like cowardly flight. Now if any questions are asked, by Ghisu or others, they will remain unanswered. Guido was lost at sea.'

'Oh, really!' She laughed, it all sounded so preposterous, and then a cold finger seemed to touch her heart, for there was a traditional sequel to a vendetta. But surely that was quite impossible? Guido might be irresponsible, but Mario was a law-abiding twentieth-century citizen.

'If ... if something *had* happened to your brother,' she hazarded, 'would you ... could you?'

He gave her an enigmatical smile. 'I get your meaning. Honestly, I don't know what I would have done. *Grazie a dio*, I shall not be tested.' He looked across towards the distant ranges. 'Although I have often hunted in the Barbagia, I would hate to have to spend the rest of my life there.'

She was answered; intuition told her that faced with the age-old demand for reprisal, Mario would react true to form. The man was completely ruthless in the pursuit of vengeance or desire. Her lips tingled as she remembered his violent lovemaking. Yet she did not feel the revulsion that she expected. She hated violence, but this man drew her like a magnet, perhaps because he was the antithesis of herself in background and upbringing, and he was magnificently male, not an effeminate fop like so many of her associates in the rag trade. However deeply he sinned, it would be on the grand scale with nothing petty about it.

She looked at him out of the corner of her eye; he was still gazingly musingly at the mountains. Suave, relaxed, impeccably groomed, his outward seeming gave no hint of the turbulent depths in the heart of his being. Loyalty, violence and secrecy were the three attributes he had ascribed to his countrymen, and he possessed them all.

He roused himself from his brooding thoughts to say lightly:

'*Ecco*, you can put all this out of your mind, for soon you will be far away and can forget our barbarism, remembering only the glitter of the Costa Smeralda.'

'That has made the least impression,' she returned. 'Does Signora Segni think as you do?'

He shrugged his shoulders. 'Presumably, since she is a Sard, though she is fast imbibing more modern ideas. I suppose *la nonna* mentioned her. My grandmother has not seen her since she has grown up and may have a shock when she does. She has acquired an advanced outlook and considers herself emancipated.'

Surprised, Lorena asked:

'But surely you don't approve of that? Don't you expect your wife to be submissive without a will of her own?'

She was becoming curious about Margherita, and it would be as well to accustom herself to the knowledge that Mario belonged to another woman.

'Certainly not. The Sardi are an independent people,' he said shortly.

'Even their women?'

'Naturally, since they are the mothers of the race.'

'But you didn't approve of my efforts to be independent,' she told him, recalling how he had objected to her proposed

91

tour of the country alone.

'You ought to be shut up,' he said deliberately. 'Loose, you are a menace to any man's peace of mind.'

That pleased her. 'Do I menace yours?' she asked provocatively.

'How could you, since I am engaged to Margherita?' he evaded her, but she saw the glint in his eyes. He pulled out the starter. 'We had better be getting back.'

Lorena felt reluctant to return to the confining atmospheres of the village, and she had found her conversation with Mario stimulating, though it had not followed the lines which she had intended it to do.

'Daren't you be alone with me any longer?' she challenged him. 'Are you afraid you might be disloyal to Margherita as you were before?' And waited breathlessly for his comeback, expecting she did not know what, but secretly hoping he would kiss her again.

He flashed a look at her which made her quail. Then almost savagely he reversed the car.

'Do not tempt me,' he said between his teeth, while his eyes smouldered. 'As a guest you are sacrosanct, but you will do well to remember that I am not one of your philandering playboys. You know you have the power to ignite me and if you drive me too far, you will get more than you bargained for. I can do much worse than I did on the boat.'

She lay back in her seat as he sent the car hurtling down the way they had come up, shattered by this glimpse of naked ferocity. Only idiots attempted to play with leopards.

CHAPTER FIVE

LUCIA greeted her grandson with restrained affection, grumbling that he had delayed visiting them for so long, though she supposed the business in Genoa had been important.

'It was,' he said shortly, but did not elucidate.

'The Signorina has fully recovered,' Lucia observed significantly, 'and wishes to be on her way.'

'I am about to arrange for her to do that,' Mario told her. 'I think she has had enough of Sardegna and the Sardi. Her holiday has not turned out quite as she expected.'

His glance challenged Lorena, but she refused to meet it, saying lightly:

'I've been glad of this opportunity to see the country as it really is.'

She looked round the rather mean room with its one window towards the street. Mario appeared to be affluent, and she wondered why he did not house the old lady with more comfort. The floor was of stone, the furniture, though strong and serviceable had neither grace nor comfort, the seats of the chairs being of hard wood, except the rocker in which Lucia was sitting.

As if sensing her thoughts, Mario said:

'My grandmother has lived all her life in this house, and refuses to move from it. Nor will she allow me to install modern amenities.'

'This was the house my bridegroom brought me to when I was wed, and I will only leave it in my coffin,' Lucia declared emphatically. 'Nor do I want comfort. Ease and luxury weaken the fibres and turn men into lapdogs.'

'I do not think I have become a lapdog,' Mario said, laughing. 'Although my own house is far from Spartan. Not only is it necessary to keep up appearances before my business colleagues, but I like to have beautiful things around me.'

'So I saw last time I visited you, but I have the hills and trees all round me, and what could be more lovely?' Lucia asked, though the view from the front of her house was only that of the grey habitations opposite to it.

She leaned towards Mario, speaking to him in the Sardo dialect which Lorena could not understand. She caught the name Guido and guessed she was enquiring about him. Assunta was busy preparing a meal and, feeling excluded, Lorena moved away to the window and stood looking out into the street.

Mario had brought in her cases, and she meditated whether she would slip away and change into something more presentable, but she feared that if she did so, he would assume that she was trying to make herself glamorous for his benefit, an idea which she did not wish to encourage. She wanted to emphasise her complete indifference to him, an indifference which she knew very well she did not feel. She found herself envying Margherita Segni.

The pattering of many feet announced that a drove of sheep was approaching. It was led by a magnificent billy-goat, with long horns and a shaggy black and white coat. He stepped proudly as if aware of his superior intelligence to the stupid flock that he was leading. There was something diabolical about goats, Lorena thought; it was their queer yellowish eyes. It was not surprising that primitive people associated them with evil.

A shepherd accompanied the animals, carrying a crook. He wore a sleeveless leather coat over his shirt and a stocking cap at a rakish angle over his black hair. A girl called to him from the house opposite, and he turned aside to speak to her.

Suddenly she saw to her dismay a small figure running towards the goat. Gigi was supposed to be playing in the

94

garden, but bored with his own company, he had come into the house, and hearing the pattering of hooves had opened the front door and run out into the street.

The goat lowered its head in a menacing manner, and without waiting to discover if it really intended to butt the child, Lorena threw open the window, scrambled over the sill and rushed to Gigi's rescue. Unheeding his protests, she picked him up and pushed him over the sill into the sitting room, expecting every moment to feel the goat's horns against her own posterior. Happily, the girl had drawn the shepherd's attention to what was happening and he ran to intercept Master Billy.

Gigi safe and herself unassaulted, Lorena made a more dignified re-entrance by the front door, to be overwhelmed by Assunta's thanks.

'*Grazie, grazie, signorina!* From the bottom of my heart I thank you.'

She saw that Mario was looking at her with surprise, but he said nothing, turning his attention to Gigi.

Lucia was sternly regarding the delinquent.

'Is it not forbidden that you go into the street alone?' she asked.

Gigi hung his head. '*Si*, Nonna.'

'Then you have been disobedient,' Mario said sternly, 'and disobedience must be punished.'

By accident or design his eyes wandered to a bunch of leather thongs hanging on the wall, which Assunta used to tie together the bundles of kindling which she collected from the hillside, and Lorena's heart quailed. If he intended to thrash the child, she would have to intervene. She could not countenance such brutality, and Mario, she knew, could be brutal, for he had treated her roughly upon occasion, and seemed to view the extermination of an enemy with equanimity.

Assunta evidently had the same thought, for she flung a protective arm round her son, crying:

'No, Mario, you shall not touch him!'

'I wasn't going to,' Mario told her mildly. 'But you cannot let disobedience pass unchallenged. That way will be disastrous to his future.'

Gigi struggled out of his mother's hold and faced Mario defiantly.

'Me want to talk to Aurelio,' he said, choosing to speak in his faulty English. 'Aurelio say I go with him to *pastori* hut. I think perhaps he forget.'

'It is much too far for your little legs,' Assunta declared firmly.

Gigi was indignant. 'My legs very strong, and Aurelio carry me or I ride on Billy.'

'So you have worked it all out,' Mario commented. 'But it is not a very good arrangement, *mio figlio*. Aurelio has his flock to manage apart from carrying you, and he seems to be a somewhat irresponsible character, more interested in girls than his duties, or he would have seen what was happening sooner.' He smiled at Lorena. 'I congratulate you upon your quickness, though perhaps it would have been wiser to let young Gigi reap the consequences of his folly— it would have taught him a lesson.'

'The goat might have hurt him,' Lorena cried. 'You ... you mustn't be hard on him, Mario'—she used his first name and Lucia raised her brows—'he's only little.'

'Not too little to be disciplined,' Mario returned inexorably. 'We have seen the result of lack of restraint in Guido.' He looked meaningly at Lucia, who smiled wanly.

'But to beat a child....' Lorena began heatedly, and Mario frowned.

'I don't beat children,' he said brusquely. 'Gigi will not go to the hut with Aurelio, that is all.'

Gigi's lip quivered. 'Please, Zio,' for so he called his cousin. 'Please, please let me go and I never bad again.'

'*Basta!*' Mario snapped. 'You do not go.' Then he relented. 'Perhaps one day soon, I will borrow a Land-Rover

96

and drive you up; as your mother says it is too far for you to walk.'

'I do not want to wait!' Gigi cried, his face crimsoning with fury. 'I want go now, with Aurelio. He nice—you horrid!'

Assunta took him firmly by the arm. 'That will do,' she said, 'or I *will* ask Zio Mario to beat you.' She led him out of the room.

'He begins to assert himself early,' Mario remarked.

Lucia chuckled. 'He has inherited the Marescu temper,' she said, 'his mother was always a handful. But it is time you had a son, Mario.'

'First I must get me a wife, Nonna.'

'Margherita is waiting,' she prompted.

He shrugged his shoulders. 'I wonder.' His glance strayed to Lorena and he sighed.

Lucia noticed both look and sigh. 'You would not marry any but a true Sard?' she said anxiously.

'Of course not, Nonna, have I not sworn it?' he returned, but he spoke almost absently. He turned to the English girl. '*Ecco, signorina*, it remains to arrange the details of your journey.'

'I'm not sure I want to be packed off just when it suits you,' Lorena retorted, needled by his calm direction of her destiny. The emphasis upon his choice of a Sardo bride had also been somehow inexplicably wounding, as if he believed all other nationalities were as faithless as his mother. She went on brightly:

'Now I've recovered my clothes and money, I don't see why I shouldn't stay on a day or two longer to see the sights ... those *nuraghes* you were talking about....'

She broke off, becoming aware that both her hearers were regarding her with hostility.

'I cannot permit you to wander about the island alone,' Mario said curtly.

'You cannot permit? Since when were you responsible

for my actions?' she asked indignantly. 'You take too much upon yourself, Signor Marescu. For the past few weeks circumstances engineered by you have forced me to obey your wishes, but now I'm a free agent I intend to do exactly what suits me.'

'Oh, no, you won't,' he returned. 'You will go on that plane from Alghero tomorrow.'

'Deporting me?' she suggested, her eyes glinting irefully. 'Is that within your powers? Be careful, or I'll report you to the authorities for forcibly detaining me.'

'That would be a poor return for our hospitality,' Lucia intervened reproachfully.

'A hospitality which I didn't seek. Oh, don't think I'm ungrateful for your care of me, but I shouldn't have been imposed upon you in the first place.'

'I entirely agree,' Lucia admitted, and looked at Mario. 'It seemed the best thing to do at the time,' he said slowly.

'No doubt it did from your point of view,' Lorena flashed. 'But you've shown me scant consideration throughout, and since you've brought my luggage, and presumably my cheques and passport are intact?' She paused interrogatively.

He stiffened. 'Why should they not be?'

'Because I believe you and your brother are capable of any crime if it suits you, and I don't think anyone could have treated me more arrogantly than you did on that boat.'

Anger and frustration had made her reckless. She desired passionately to break the cool indifference of his voice and manner, and she saw with satisfaction his face darken with fury.

'*Signorina*,' Lucia protested, 'no one speaks to Mario like that in my house.'

Mario told her: 'Nonna, please leave us. I wish to put the Signorina right about a few facts.' He was controlling his temper with difficulty.

'You needn't bother,' Lorena flashed. 'I've nothing more to say to you. I'm going to my room.'

'No, you are not.' His hand closed around her wrist like a steel handcuff. 'Please, Nonna.'

The old woman rose from the rocking chair and walked with dignity to the door, turning back to say:

'I hope you are going to beat her, Mario, it is what she deserves.'

The door closed behind her.

'You ... you wouldn't dare?' Lorena gasped. The Sard's expression indicated that he was quite capable of carrying out his grandmother's suggestion, and she felt an uneasy qualm. That would be an indignity too great to be borne.

'It is not a question of daring,' he returned, 'but we haven't reached that degree of intimacy ... yet. Sit down.'

He pushed her on to one of the hard chairs and released her wrist. She rubbed it mechanically, thinking it would show a bruise. The man's sinewy brown fingers had not been gentle.

He took his stance before her, black brows drawn over glittering dark eyes.

'Now you listen to me. You stowed yourself away on my boat for reasons known only to yourself, which placed me in an extremely awkward position. Not content with that, you panicked in that squall, running up on deck in an idiotic manner, which caused you to knock yourself out. Let me tell you it is not easy to steer a boat in a storm and deal with an injured woman at the same time. I have already explained why I brought you here, though you seem too dim to grasp the necessity. After these misadventures, I should have thought you would be glad to leave the country, unless...' His eyes narrowed intently. 'You are regretting Giulio?'

'Of course not.' But the fire had gone out of her with the knowledge that he considered her a nuisance and was longing to see the last of her.

'I am sure you should be getting back to that important work of yours,' he said sarcastically. 'And considering all the trouble you've caused us, I don't think I am asking too much of you.'

'I can't stay here any longer, but I don't see why I should be hounded out of the country because I'm an embarrarass-ment to you,' she said rebelliously. She nearly added 'Like Guido', but checked herself in time; that she knew would be unforgivable. 'I've a good mind to go to the *carabinieri* tell them you kidnapped me.'

'Kidnappers demand a ransom,' he returned with a fleet-ing smile. 'I have asked nothing of you.'

'No, you took what you wanted,' she flung at him, and then blushed, wishing she had bitten out her tongue before she had reminded him of that wild embrace, which he had indicated he regretted.

'Not all by any means.' His smile became sardonic. 'And you did not exactly resist me.'

'I must have been mad,' she murmured, her colour in-creasing. 'No one has ever dared to treat me like that be-fore.'

'You surprise me. Your admirers must have been singu-larly unenterprising,' he gibed. 'But enough, you will be ready to leave tomorrow afternoon.'

'And if I'm not?'

He looked at the thongs on the wall.

'I am beginning to think Nonna was right and I shall have to take a strap to you.'

Her eyes glinted up at his forbidding face.

'Is that a Sardo practice? To beat their women into sub-mission?'

'Do you think either my grandmother or Assunta are subdued?'

'No, but they seem to hold you in some awe.' She mim-icked Lucia's voice. 'Nobody speaks to Mario like that in my house.' The imitation was very good, she even caught

100

the slightly American intonation, and for the fraction of a second as he took a step towards her, she thought that she had gone too far.

There was a red light in his eyes and his hands came out to grasp her. She shrank back, bracing herself against a wooden chair back to meet his onslaught, but he checked himself, and moved away to the window. He stood with his back to her staring out at the street, but his hands were clenched.

Lorena relaxed slowly, her eyes fixed upon his long, lithe figure, crowned with inky hair, and wondered what devil had got into her, for she had desired his embrace. That was crazy. He was betrothed to another girl and he was the last man with whom she should fall in love. She was not in love with him, she assured herself feverishly, at least only a little, but even while she reasoned with herself, a surge of intense emotion rose within her. She wanted to cry out—'Beat me. Do what you like with me, but don't send me away from you.' With an effort she quelled the wild impulse. What was there about this man that could arouse her so violently? Until she had met him, she had always been so sure of herself, and had regarded the women who made fools of themselves over men with contemptuous pity. In a civilised age they should have more control, she considered, for never having experienced the force of strong passion herself, she could not understand that it could become all compelling.

She realised it now, but recognised its folly. If Mario took her, he would use her and throw her away, despising her weakness. So the cry of her heart went unuttered and she waited in quivering silence for his next words.

He turned back from the window, and now he was completely master of himself, his unclenched hands hanging at his sides.

'You are a provoking little witch,' he told her, softening the words with his brilliant smile. 'It will be a good thing

101

for ... both of us when you are safely on that plane tomorrow. If you had any sense, you would realise that yourself.'

He strode to the door while she wilted under his words. 'Be ready when I come for you,' he commanded. *'Ciao.'* He went out, slamming the door behind him.

Lorena felt a flicker of triumph. He was afraid of her, afraid that she might tempt him from his allegiance to Margherita. But what was the good of that, since he was determined to put her out of his life? After tomorrow she would never see him again. Her moment of exultation was drowned in a wave of desolation.

The midday meal, which Mario would not stay to attend, was served very late owing to the events of the morning. It was eaten almost in silence. Gigi was sulking, Assunta seemed preoccupied, and though Lucia attempted conversational remarks appertaining to Lorena's departure on the morrow, she soon gave up the effort, for the English girl was not responsive.

Pasta was served, ewes' milk cheese, and the loaves of *carta da musica*, bread made of Sardo corn in rounds like plates, which crackled when broken, the sound being the suggested origin of its name. The meal concluded, Lorena went to change her clothes.

She was relieved to discover that her money and papers were intact; not that she thought for one moment that Mario would have tampered with them, but other people might have had access to her belongings during her absence. Her wrist watch too had been retrieved from her beach bag. Venetia had made a neat job of the packing, but she had sent no message.

Lorena was still tempted to defy Mario's instructions, though she could stay no longer an unwelcome guest in that house. She could go elsewhere. As he had said it was time that she took up her old life again, after a brief visit home to reassure her parents, but an extra day or two was neither here nor there, and she was loath to submit to the Sard's dictation.

She derived considerable comfort from the exchange into her own clothes. Her well cut slacks and smart shirt did much to restore her morale, which had been sapped by Assunta's ill-fitting skirt. For the first time since the expedition to the caves, she was able to make up her face, a proceeding which she afterwards regretted, for when she reappeared, Assunta glanced at her eye-shadow and lipstick with lifted brows, and Lucia remarked sourly that Mario did not care for paint.

'But he has gone,' Lorena said sweetly. 'And make-up is part of my uniform, so to speak.'

'It is wasted upon the villagers,' Lucia grumbled. 'They will think you are Jezebel.'

And not only them, Lorena thought wryly, as she went into the garden to play with Gigi. He, however, was not responsive; he was still lowering about his cousin's rebuke and not being allowed to go with Aurelio, and kept muttering threats below his breath.

'If I had knife I would kill Zio Mario,' he said once.

Lorena scolded him, but without much effect. She was seeing the Sardo temperament in the raw, she thought, vengeful and vindictive. Lucia had said Mario had been just such another.

She still could not make up her mind what she intended to do upon the morrow, and when she went to bed she tried to concentrate upon a plan of action, but her thoughts kept reverting to Mario. The man's proud, sombre face kept coming before her mental vision, distracting her.

She had never been seriously involved with a man, never gone beyond light flirtation. She had not wanted to marry, her work absorbed her, and she knew her career was not compatible with matrimony. Before she seriously contemplated marriage, she must meet someone who would sweep her off her feet, as the saying was, make her believe that

103

love was the most important thing in her life. She had thought it unlikely that any man could until she had met Mario. In his arms she had experienced an upsurging of her senses of which she had not believed herself capable. Instinctively she knew that he could make her forget that she had ever considered her work important. But he despised and scorned her, though she knew she attracted him, albeit against his will. He scorned himself even more than he did her for being attracted. Yet, even if things were otherwise, what chance of happiness would she have with him? He was a man of different standards, different nationality, of a fierce, jealous disposition which would be unendurable to live with, or so she insisted to herself, well aware that it was a case of sour grapes, for he was betrothed to another girl.

Mario could never be anything to her, and it was as well that she would see him no more after tomorrow. She recognised that her wish to stay on in Sardinia was motivated by her reluctance to leave his vicinity. When at last she fell asleep she had decided to be wise and fall in with his arrangements.

In the morning Lorena went to the bank to change some of her travellers' cheques in preparation for her journey. Gigi wanted to accompany her, but Assunta vetoed that, apparently fearing that he would elude her en route. This resulted in another row, with Gigi being confined to the room which he shared with his mother.

Lorena was sorry about that, but there was nothing she could do. She bought a small present to leave for him when she finally went. She returned to the house to deposit it and her handbag in her room, and feeling restless went out again into the bright sunshine, finding it difficult to realise that this was the last day she would spend in the village.

She wandered about the streets, noticing her trousers were causing whispered comments among the older men sitting on the steps of their houses, wearing the ugly modern invention of a cloth cap, in place of the stocking ones of their fathers, which were so much more becoming. This irritated her a little; surely they had seen women in pants before? She understood there were tourist expeditions to the village in the season, but this corner of the island was so backward, they could not alter their ideas. She remembered the other more sinister traditions which still lingered there, and shivered. Perhaps she was not altogether sorry to be leaving it.

The one or two younger men she encountered were frankly admiring, but no one attempted to accost her. Mario had said the Sards were always courteous to women.

One old man she saw was wearing the traditional dress, which was seldom seen except at festivals, a magpie affair of white shirt, full white pantaloons thrust into boots, a sort of black garment coming half way down his thighs which was neither trousers nor kilt, together with a sleeveless black sheepskin jacket and a stocking cap. His face was nut brown and deeply seamed with wrinkles caused by age and toil. Lorena smiled at him, but he turned his head away as if her appearance offended him.

There were women too doing their marketing, the old ones wearing long pleated wool skirts and black shawls, the few young ones in abbreviated modern skirts and blouses. They looked at her with unconcealed curiosity. Several stopped her and attempted to talk. She was a *turista*, was she not? How did she like Sardinia? Was she staying long? Lorena answered them politely and somewhat vaguely. She could not be too explicit about how she came to be there.

She regretted that she had had no opportunity to see a festival when the villagers wore their regional costumes, which Assunta had told her were exceedingly beautiful, and would be much more becoming, she thought, to the dark Sardo girls than their efforts at modern styling.

Reluctantly she returned to the house with the intention of repacking her cases ready for Mario's advent in the

105

afternoon. Assunta met her at the door and her face creased with anxiety when she saw she was alone.

'I hoped Gigi was with you,' she said. 'Have you seen him?'

'No. You forbade him to come with me.'

'But you come in and go out again. I thought he might have run after you.' Assunta looked really worried. 'I lock him in our room because he defy me. He climb out of window and down by the creepers. *Madonna mia*, it is time we go back to Rome and *mio padre* can take him in hand. He grow too much for me.'

'He can't have gone far,' Lorena said.

'He go to find Aurelio,' Assunta told her. 'He go up with the sheep this morning.' She looked at the sun. 'By now they far away. *Dio mio*, what can I do?' She wrung her hands, becoming truly Latin in her agitation. '*La nonna* is in a fret about him. He is to her the apple of the eye. I dare not leave her alone. She might have another heart attack.'

'I could go after him,' Lorena offered, 'if you tell me where they will have gone.'

'Will you? Aurelio make for the hut, but with Gigi, I do not think he go fast. You will overtake them ... but you leave this afternoon, you have things to do, perhaps?'

'Gigi is more important,' Lorena told her.

Possibly Gigi was not with the shepherd, but it seemed more than probable, and Lorena had little difficulty in persuading Assunta to let her start in pursuit. She had much rather go after him than be left to cope with Lucia. Assunta described the route; past the church she would find a rough track ascending the hills, she could not miss it as it was the only one. The hut was a long way off in the uplands, but Assunta was confident that Lorena would come upon the truant long before he arrived there.

'Aurelio very bad not to tell me,' she said, 'but he think Gigi had the permission. It is most good of you, Lorena, but I know you are good as bread, whatever *la nonna* and

106

Mario say.'

Lorena winced at this frank remark.

'Even Mario doesn't question my good nature, only my morals,' she said drily, 'and I'm glad to be able to do something in return for all you've done for me.'

She set off briskly downhill towards the church, and had no difficulty in finding the winding track beyond it which Assunta had described.

It was a warm sunny morning with for once no wind. Heat haze obscured the distant hills, dew still spangled the blackberry blossom's drapery of cobwebs, and bird song shook the air with trilling notes, but after the first few furlongs, without a sign of her quarry, Lorena became too tired to appreciate the beauties of the scenery.

It was rough walking and her sandals were quite inadequate, giving no protection to her burning feet. The route was a dusty, winding track, passing between dry stretches of *macchia* and through groves of oak and chestnut, all the time rising steadily upwards.

Lorena paused and looked back. The village had shrunk to a grey line beneath the mountain crest. Surely she should have overtaken the shepherd by now? Perhaps he had travelled faster than Assunta had surmised. She could not suppose Gigi had walked so far, but she remembered he had talked about Aurelio carrying him, or being mounted upon a goat. Perhaps she had better press on until she came upon the hut which was apparently their destination. She would find Aurelio there, even if Gigi were not with him, and could satisfy herself upon that point.

She came out on to rolling uplands, where animals were grazing, and thought she recognised the black and white goat. So she was on the right trail, Aurelio must have left his flock and be seeking refreshment in the hut; he would need it after that trek, she thought.

She paused by a mountain stream to drink and lave her hot face and hands. Rolling up her trousers, she dabbled her

107

feet in it. Refreshed, she resumed her sandals, now sadly scuffed, and continued her upward climb.

Haze obliterated the sun, and there was no breeze at all, signs she was too inexperienced to interpret. Far below the valleys were still bathed in sunlight, with a theatrical effect. The track ended at a steep bank, up which a narrow path climbed in zigzags. Lorena toiled up it, wondering how many miles she had walked.

At the top of the bank was a small level space with a stream running across it. Beyond it were further rolling fells, while to her right, a rugged outcrop of rock formed the bastion of a mountain approach.

There under its lee she saw the hut, protected by an overhang of rock and surrounded by blackberry bushes, a tiny primitive edifice constructed of unmortared stone.

The air was very still, and on the little plateau there was no living thing, not even a browsing sheep or goat; the birds and insects had fallen silent.

Lorena went up to the ramshackle building, and knocked upon the door, calling: 'Gigi! Aurelio!'

There was no reply, so she pushed it open, looking around. The interior was bigger than its outside suggested, but the furnishings were very crude. At one end a stone apparatus, filled with kindling, was apparently the cooking stove, with a hole in the roof for a chimney. There were a couple of wooden stools and a bench ran along one wall covered with several sheepskins, presumably the bed. The floor was beaten earth, the fourth wall was the living rock, with crevices in it which did duty for cupboards. There were signs of recent occupation, cooking utensils round the fireplace, water in a crock, but there was no indication of Gigi's presence.

She sat down on the bench; at least the sheepskins were soft to her weary limbs, and she hoped they were clean. Her ears were alert for approaching footsteps, but utter stillness continued to reign outside.

She looked at her watch and saw it was long past midday. Mario was coming to fetch her that afternoon, and she pictured his wrath when he found her absent with some amusement. She had a perfectly valid excuse for her truancy, so he could not really blame her. By the time she got back to the village it would be too late to travel to Alghero today, she thought with satisfaction.

She had only had a light breakfast, and her long walk had made her ravenously hungry. Since Aurelio and Gigi had not put in an appearance, she sought among the crocks for something edible, sure that her absent hosts would not grudge her that. Even the humblest Sard was hospitable. She looked into an iron pot, which had a chain to hang it over the fire, and found it contained some sort of stew, but it was cold and the fire was out. She replaced the lid, and discovered wrapped in a clean cloth a bone with some meat upon it. This she gnawed with appetite. She needed some sustenance before she started the long trek back.

This was certainly life in the raw, she thought ruefully, looking at her greasy fingers, and she was becoming convinced that her efforts had been all for nothing, as it seemed more and more apparent that Gigi had not come up here at all. If he had, surely Aurelio would have left him in the hut, for the child must have been exhausted by the time they got there. He must have taken refuge from his mother's displeasure with one of the neighbours and was probably home by now. Reluctantly she stood up. She would wash her hands in the stream and begin her journey back; at least it would be downhill.

She went outside and was appalled by what she saw.

Mist was rolling down over the northern landscape, a sea fog creeping in from the coast. It was like a grey blanket obliterating hills and forests, and the air had become very chill, the sun was veiled, and the valley up which she had come was already filling up with vapour. She looked at her watch, calculating how long it had taken her to reach the hut, and realised that however much she hurried, it would be dusk before she arrived, and in the dark and fog she might easily lose her way. In that desolate region she could stumble about all night without coming upon a habitation, and would run the risk of falling over an escarpment.

She decided that she had better stay where she was. Here she had cover of a sort, and if Assunta organised a search party, they would know where to find her. Aurelio might appear at any moment and would guide her down in safety. Surely he too would need shelter, and possibly also some of his colleagues. They would be astonished to see her, and she hoped she would be able to explain what had happened.

She drank from the stream and washed her hands inadequately in the running water, wondering if the *pastori* used soap, or if they did not bother with ablutions, probably the latter. Wisps of mist were creeping over the plateau, and she went back into the hut, glad of its inhospitable shelter, drawing the sheepskins about her for warmth.

Her situation had some points of resemblance with her predicament aboard the boat, but this time there was no likelihood of encountering Mario. He would be very angry with her for disorganising his plans and was quite capable of believing that she had used Gigi's disappearance as a means of thwarting them, especially if the boy had turned up in the meantime, as she was hopeful that he had. Mario would consider that a night in the hut was only her just deserts. Had he not been ready to expose Gigi to the goat's horns to teach him a lesson? He was vindictive and cruel, she thought viciously, for she was still smarting from the humiliation which he had heaped upon her. Whatever he said to the contrary he was capable of carrying on any number of vendettas if his pride was involved. Her own relationship with him was something in the nature of a feud, and he would not miss this opportunity of extracting his revenge.

What was it he had called her? The epitome of the beautician's and the couturier's arts. It would appeal to his sardonic humour to think of her benighted in a shepherd's hut with no amenities whatever.

She settled herself on the bench among the sheepskins, and being exhausted by her long trek, she began to doze, and presently was fast asleep.

She dreamed and dreamed fearfully, one of those nightmares in which the sleeper is pursued by some nameless terror and the feet seem weighted with lead.

She awoke in a sweat of terror and her surroundings were a continuation of her dream. It was dark and something wet and clammy seemed to enshroud her face, which she could not brush aside. Then she saw approaching her a gleaming eye of some beast or demon. Though not normally a screamer, she gave a strangled shriek.

The eye disappeared, but strong arms enfolded her, holding her closely against a body which was comfortingly human. She clung to it, sobbing hysterically, while its owner whispered soothing words.

Being only half awake, she thought, as she had done during her illness, that it was her father who was holding her, for so often when she had been a child he had soothed her night terrors, coming to her when she had cried out, stroking her hair and telling her gently that the bogeys had all gone away.

'I had such a horrid dream. . . .' she whispered.

'You are awake now,' a soft voice murmured. 'And quite safe with me. There . . . don't cry.' A handkerchief smelling of lavender wiped her face, and she snuggled closer to the comforting shoulder, while its owner's hand gently caressed her head.

Gradually she grew calmer and her perceptions sharpening, she remembered where she was. Her rescuer could not be her father, who was far away in England, nor was the voice whispering those reassuring words her father's voice. The man who was holding her was Mario.

With a sudden twist she wrenched herself out of his arms and drew away from him to the farthest limit of the bench. Impenetrable darkness lay between them.

'You!' she exclaimed. 'You!'

He said, and his voice sounded unsteady: 'You have a proclivity for landing yourself in perilous situations, *cara mia*.'

'Has Gigi been found?' she asked anxiously.

'*Si*, he did not go with Aurelio after all. Assunta should have made sure before she sent you off on such a wild goose chase. She was much concerned when I arrived and you had not returned, and so she should be. Since my car cannot get up here, I borrowed a Land-Rover and came to retrieve you.'

She laughed shakily. 'And I thought you would think my predicament would serve me right.'

'How could you think that?' he said reproachfully. 'Indeed, we owe you gratitude for risking so much discomfort for the child. But I'm afraid your ordeal is not over yet.'

'What ... what do you mean?'

'That the fog shows no signs of lifting and because of it, I ran off the track and the Land-Rover is bogged down in a morass. You do choose your moments, don't you? Fogs and squalls.'

'I'm not lucky in my weather,' she remarked, trying to reconcile Mario's behaviour with her previous conceptions of him. Then as the full significance of what he had told her made its impact, she exclaimed with dismay:

'You don't mean we shall have to spend the night here?'

She heard him laugh, and now all tenderness had fled and it held a note of mockery.

'Exactly so, *carina mia*,' he said softly. 'Exactly so.'

CHAPTER SIX

'HISTORY repeats itself—history repeats itself.' The adage reiterated in Lorena's tired brain. For the second time since coming to the island, she was alone with this exciting and unpredictable man in an equivocal position.

The first time she had been an unwelcome stowaway, but this time he had voluntarily come to her rescue. The rescue unfortunately had gone awry with the ditching of the Land-Rover—she could hardly credit that he had done that on purpose, since he had shown very plainly that he wanted to be rid of her.

Now fate had thrown them together and they would be alone through the long night hours, and there was nothing to stop him from yielding to temptation and taking advantage of them. Nothing but her own resolution. She had learned more about him since that night on the boat, and she was not going to play second string to Margherita Segni. He might think she was of no account, but she would not let him cheapen her again. If he wanted fun while Margherita made up her mind, or whatever was delaying their nuptials, he was not going to have it with Lorena Lawrence.

Out of the darkness, he suggested: 'Suppose we try to make ourselves a little more comfortable?'

He fumbled for the torch which she had mistaken for some creature's eye when he came in, and finding it, shone it round the hut. It was full of swirling mist, which was what she had felt on her face. Depending from the roof was a lantern, which she had not noticed before. It contained a candle, and when he lit it, it only gave a feeble glimmer in the shrouded room. He went to the door and closed it. A shiver of apprehension ran up Lorena's spine. He and she were shut in alone.

He turned his attention to the fire, setting a match to the kindling in the stone grate. It flared up and he piled logs upon it, which emitted a puff of smoke to mingle with the fog. Then it burned with a steady blaze and gradually the room started to clear.

'What can have happened to Aurelio and his pals?' she asked. 'Won't they be using this place tonight?'

She would have welcomed the arrival of the shepherds to break the tension which she sensed was already mounting between them.

He shrugged his shoulders. 'Probably dossing with the sheep, on a higher pasture. They will not be coming down as late as this.'

'But I can't stay here all night with you,' she said desperately, for vivid in her mind was what happened last time they had been alone at night. The memory set her pulses hammering, but that was a madness to which she must not succumb.

Even in the dim light she saw his sardonic smile.

'Experiencing some belated sense of the proprieties?' he enquired. 'But at least this time you are fully clothed.'

She sprang up from the bench. 'I'm going,' she announced, and grabbing the torch made for the door.

Quick as she was, he was faster. He stood before the door, barring her exit, a dark, menacing figure.

'You will do no such thing. Don't be so silly, Lorena. Sit down and make the best of the situation.'

She threw up her head defiantly and his brows drew together ominously.

'I do not want to have to use any rough stuff,' he said warningly. 'It would be bad for both of us, so please be sensible.'

She sat down again on the bench, aware that her limbs were trembling.

'That is better,' he approved. 'You must reconcile your-

114

self to being marooned until daylight. Suppose you try to go to sleep again.'

'I don't think I can,' she told him, wondering if he had really comforted her, or if it had been part of her dream. 'And what will you do?'

His lips twitched into a wicked smile. 'I daresay that bench would accommodate us both.'

'Oh!' She shrank back, her eyes wide with fear. 'No. Please!'

'*Basta*,' he said roughly. 'You can trust me. I do not intend to take advantage of the situation. You can sleep in peace.'

He looked at the fire which was dying down.

'We need more fuel. Doubtless there is some stacked outside. Will you promise not to move while I fetch it?'

'And if I won't?'

He said patiently: 'I am not going to touch you, and at least you can be warm and sheltered here, but if you persist in being unreasonable, I will not be answerable for the consequences—do you understand?' His eyes were smouldering as they so often did when he looked at her. 'It is hard enough to keep my hands off you without any added provocation,' he told her shortly.

Again a quiver of excitement ran up her spine.

'Very well, I promise,' she said meekly, not finding his last utterance exactly reassuring.

He went out, closing the door behind him. Obeying a wild impulse to escape, Lorena ran to it and opened it a crack, to find pitch darkness outside; the beam of light from the door barely penetrating the thick veil of mist. She had no option but to stay where she was.

She went back to the bench and sat down, realising she was very tired and not a little hungry. She hoped Mario would behave himself, she did not feel equal to contending with him if he became amorous and it would be an unequal battle. She recalled how she had clung to him, believing he was her father. He had been different then, gentle, almost tender while he had soothed her. No wonder that she had not immediately recognised him. But as soon as she had recovered herself, he had reverted to his usual mocking insolence and wounding insinuations. Did he show that other side to the girl to whom he was plighted? If so she must find him irresistible. As for herself, he concealed it from her because he considered her to be a cheap hussy, and she had connived to give him that impression. She gave a long sigh. In other circumstances he might have respected, even loved her. . . . She checked her thoughts sharply; of what use if he were promised to someone else?

He came in carrying a mountain of logs, kicking the door open, and depositing his load on the hearth. He went back to fasten the door, carefully avoiding looking at her. His bulk and presence seemed to fill the little room.

'Have you had any food?' he asked abruptly.

'I found a knuckle bone which I chewed, but that was a long time ago.'

He laughed. 'The elegant fashion model gnawing a bone —that must have been a sight worth seeing!' She smiled wryly, the same thought having occurred to her.

'You are learning how the other half of the world lives,' he went on, 'but I don't want to starve you.'

He, as she had done, began to search among the crocks. 'If I know the *pastori*, they will have something in store.' He came upon the iron pot and gave a grunt of satisfaction. Lifting it, he suspended it from a hook above the fire.

'Mutton broth,' he told her. 'Most sustaining. They kill their own meat. This was probably an ailing lamb.'

'Oh, don't!'

'If you are sufficiently hungry, you will not be fussy.'

A savoury smell came from the pot, and Lorena stifled her qualms.

'You seem to know your way about,' she remarked, as he delved into what appeared to be a hole in the rock wall and

116

produced wooden spoons and bowls.

'This is not the first time I have spent a night in this hut,' he informed her. 'I have often stopped here on my way to and from the mountains on hunting expeditions. Much of the land hereabouts belongs to the Marescus.'

'Does farming here pay?' she asked with the interest of a farmer's daughter.

'Not the sort of money you would need,' he told her with a mocking smile. 'It is not as profitable as the Costa Smeralda.'

'I can do without luxury,' she assured him earnestly. 'Often I feel drawn to the simple life.'

He lifted the pot off the fire.

'That is not the same thing as having to live it,' he pointed out. 'No doubt you fancy it for a change, but consider, it entails no Paris gowns, no exotic food, no expensive cars.'

He began to fill the bowls.

'But you don't live it yourself,' she protested. 'You are dressed by a good tailor and possess a big car.'

He shot her an oblique glance.

'You are very observant,' he drawled. 'But I have acquired other assets with which to indulge my expensive tastes.'

She wondered what they were. She had gained the impression that he was not very proud of them; perhaps he thought it was wrong to be well off when many of his countrymen were so poor.

He handed her a bowl of the steaming mess and one of the wooden spoons, saying *'Buon appetito,'* which was the customary courtesy when a waiter set a plate before a customer, with a quirk of his black brows.

Lorena swallowed it gratefully, finding it as appetising as it smelt.

'That,' she said, putting down her empty bowl, 'was more welcome than the finest caviare.'

'Real hunger savours the meanest dish.'

She settled herself in her nest of sheepskins, feeling comfortably warm and replete. What her situation would have been if Mario had not found her, she shuddered to think. He was sitting on one of the stools, his back against the rock wall. He was wearing a black pullover with dark trousers, which made him look slim and athletic. He did not seem to know how to dispose of his long legs.

'I feel mean having the only bed,' she said with compunction.

'Is that an invitation?' he drawled.

'No!' she exclaimed hastily.

He laughed. 'Go to sleep.'

She lay for a long time watching his dark face illuminated by the glow from the fire. From time to time he threw on another log, then resumed his brooding stare, his habitual expression of sombre pride. She wondered of what he was thinking; his face revealed nothing and he seemed to have gone a hundred miles away from her. Was he thinking of Margherita Segni? Did he love the Sardo girl, or was it, as had been implied, an arranged marriage? The last, she thought, was more likely. If he did love, he would be overwhelming, but he was not a man who would ever allow his heart to lead him into an alliance with a foreigner. After the disaster of his father's marriage, he had sworn never to make the same mistake. Then, realising where her thoughts were tending, she flushed in the darkness, and presently fell asleep.

When she awoke, she was alone in the hut. The door had been set ajar, and the early morning sunshine was pouring in; the mist had been dispersed by a slight breeze.

Stiff and cramped from her hard bed, Lorena struggled to her feet and went outside, wondering what had become of Mario. In the clear morning light every detail in the valleys beneath her stood out clearly, while to the south and east, beyond the wooded hump of the hill in the shelter of which the hut was situated, the blue lines of the distant ranges were visible.

The breeze brought to her the scent of herbs and flowers and was invigorating after the closeness of the hut and the humidity of the previous day. She knelt by the clear, cold water of the stream and bathed her face and hands.

A troop of black pigs came rootling through the scrub towards the plateau of green turf on which she knelt, a sow with her train of piglets. She stopped in dismay at sight of the trespasser, her nose wrinkling, as she got her scent. Then with a grunt of disgust, she headed back into cover, her youngest offspring squealing indignantly at this change of direction.

Lorena laughed at this porcine interlude, then she unplaited her hair, shaking it loose. She had a comb in her pocket to deal with its tangles. Through its meshes she caught sight of a figure standing beside the hut, not Mario, but the shepherd, Aurelio, his hand raised against the sun to shield his eyes while he observed her.

He evidently thought that she was a creature from another sphere, for he crossed himself vigorously, then extended his fingers in the gesture which she knew was meant to ward off the evil eye.

Then Mario emerged from behind the blackberry bushes. That he too had been performing his ablutions was obvious from his wet hair. He had taken off his pullover and his shirt was open at the neck, exposing his brown muscular throat. He had been unable to shave and his chin was blue, giving him a slightly villainous look. Feeling a little light-headed, Lorena giggled.

'Enter the chief brigand,' she said.

'That is unfair,' he complained, smiling. 'I have treated you like a ... gentleman.'

'So you did ... this time,' she admitted.

He turned his attention to the waiting Aurelio, who was obviously astonished to see him, and touched his brow with a gesture of deference. Mario looked anything but pleased to see the shepherd, but he addressed him civilly in his dialect. The man replied, his small dark eyes wandering from one to the other of them, while a knowing gleam shone in them. Mario frowned, and made some further statement. Aurelio bowed to them both and bounded away.

'He says there is some coffee and sugar in the hut, so we had better try to manufacture some breakfast,' Mario told her, 'though I am afraid it will not be very appetising.'

He seemed preoccupied and kept eyeing her speculatively. She wondered what the shepherd had said to annoy him.

They went into the hut and Mario started up the fire again. From a recess he produced an ancient iron kettle which he filled with water from the crock. The place had more amenities than she had suspected. From various recesses which looked like holes in the rock he extracted coffee and bread, the *carta da musica*, which did not go stale. From outside they heard the sound of bleating, and ran out to ascertain its cause.

By the door lay a heap of shining fish, and a goat with a full udder was tied to a ring in the hut wall. Aurelio must have brought them while they were busy inside, and had rushed away again to escape their thanks.

'Fresh trout!' Mario exclaimed with satisfaction. 'That is an offering worth having. He must have caught them at dawn.' He looked doubtfully at the goat. 'That I suppose is our morning milk, but I am afraid we will have to drink our coffee black.' He picked up the fish and looked at Lorena quizzically. 'I don't imagine for one moment that you know how to deal with these?'

'I do, but it is not a chore I'm partial to,' she returned. 'If you'll clean the fish, I'll deal with nanny.'

He looked stupefied. 'You can milk?'

'One of my lesser skills. Haven't I mentioned that I'm a farmer's daughter? Of course milking is done by machinery, but I learned how to do it by hand for fun.'

'You really are a surprising person, Lorena.'

'I told you once you didn't know me,' she reminded him, 'but you're becoming better acquainted with me.'

'I certainly am,' he announced significantly.

He walked down to the stream with the fish, while Lorena fetched a wooden bucket and stool from the hut. She stroked the animal's neck to establish good relations, and sat down by the goat, proceeding to strip her. The operation was soothing to both of them, and Lorena was full of new hope. Was Mario revising his estimation of her? It would be nice to know that she was leaving behind her a pleasanter impression than the one he had hitherto held of her.

She supposed that later in the day he would take her back to the village and thence on to the airport and that would be that. The bustle of the air terminal seemed very remote from this pastoral setting, where time seemed to have stood still. They had yet to negotiate their return, and she wondered if the Land-Rover was much damaged and they would have to walk, but that would be a pleasure in Mario's company.

The goat stripped, Lorena released her and she trotted away to rejoin her mates, as Mario came back with the fish.

It was a wonderful meal eaten in the open air. The fish, which had been grilled over the red ashes of the fire, tasted delicious, the café au lait was augmented with the rich goat's milk. Lorena was blissfully happy, living in the now with Mario's presence beside her. He was in one of his best moods, describing adolescent adventures experienced in the country round about them, when he had lived with his grandmother. Apparently money had been tight, the revenue from his father's lands was small.

'That was before I struck lucky,' he told her with a wry smile. But he did not say in what way, and again she re-

121

ceived the impression that he was not proud of the source of his good fortune. She did not presume to question him, since it was no concern of hers. He did not mention Margherita.

While he talked, Lorena was aware that he was studying her closely, and when they had finished their meal, he said awkwardly:

'I must apologise to you, Lorena. I do not think that you are the little go-getter which I mistook you for. No selfish sybarite would act as you have done with Gigi, rescuing him from the goat, coming all the way up here, and last night you behaved with ... er ... circumspection.' He cleared his throat, looking embarrassed. 'Always I had difficulty in reconciling you with that frivolous crowd you were staying with, you seemed ... different.' He gesticulated with his hands. 'I am very sorry that I misjudged you.'

'Appearances were against me,' she admitted, while a surge of happiness swept through her. So at last his misconceptions with regard to her had blown away. She raised her eyes to his in a clear, candid gaze, they were limpid and pure as a grey sea on a cloudy day, and said earnestly: 'I'm not the mercenary little flirt that you believed me to be.'

'Then why did you try to throw dust into my eyes?'

'Well, at first it was too much bother to try to undeceive you, you were so determined to think the worst of me.' He winced, and she dimpled. 'After that I went on out of ... mischief.'

'Mischief!' he exclaimed, his brows drawing together. '*Dio mio*, I'd like to wring your neck!'

'Always the violent Sard!'

He looked abashed. 'I am not really a violent man, Lorena, except when I am provoked.'

'That I've noticed.'

'Could not fail to, could you?' he grinned, and was instantly sober again. 'I have not treated you with respect,'

He sounded distressed.

'Who bothers about that?' she asked lightly.

'I do,' he told her emphatically.

'Oh well, no doubt as you say I provoked your ... er ... little lapses,' she excused him. 'But I'll forgive you.'

'Had I not misunderstood you there would have been no little lapses, as you call them,' he said seriously, 'delightful though they were.' He stared at her wonderingly. 'But you did not repulse me as you should have done,' he added accusingly.

Though the hot colour flooded her face, she did not drop her eyes, and said with perfect honesty:

'To be truthful, Mario, no man has ever moved me like you did. I ... I didn't know I could behave ... as I did.'

She saw triumph shine in his eyes.

'So you were like the sleeping beauty when I woke you with my kiss?'

'There was more than one,' she murmured wickedly. 'Well ... er ... yes, I suppose your poetic way of putting it was what happened.'

'But you must have been kissed before,' he insisted. 'I know your casual British ways.'

'Of course, but it never meant anything to me, and I never permitted ... I mean they were only experimental, and ... er ... disappointing.'

He laughed gleefully. 'And my kisses were not?'

Feeling she was betraying much too much, Lorena said sedately:

'That's enough of the subject. We've both made the *amende honorable* and we will leave it at that. Do you still intend to pack me off to Rome?'

He began to pick aimlessly at the grass beside him.

'That is as you please.'

'What a concession! I confess there are a few things I'd like to see before I go.'

'Then I will be your guide.'

Her heart leaped and sank. It would not do, she told herself desperately. In his company she would only become more deeply involved and there was nothing for her in his direction. He had said in her presence that he had sworn to marry a Sard, so even if the bond to Margherita could be broken, he would never turn to her.

'We'll have to see about that,' she said coolly, 'but our immediate problem is how to get back to the village. Incidentally, what'll they think about us being out all night?'

'Nothing very charitable,' he said grimly.

'They must realise it wasn't our fault,' she pointed out. 'Suppose you go and see if you can do anything with the Land-Rover while I wash up these platters.'

'Leave them for Aurelio to do.'

'I couldn't dream of doing that, especially as he provided such an excellent breakfast.'

Mario hesitated, seemed about to speak, then changed his mind and strode away to investigate the Land-Rover, but Lorena was deprived of her chores, for Aurelio appeared out of nowhere and with nods and smiles, took the vessels out of her hands. She surmised Mario must have noticed him hovering and that was why he had not said what was on his mind. She caught the shepherd staring at her curiously, and wondered what Mario had said to him when he had found them together in the early morning. Something in his expression made her feel uncomfortable. Murmuring '*Addio*,' she ran off to discover how Mario was faring with their transport.

The vehicle was some way down the track, and she found him hot and dishevelled, trying to dislodge its front wheels from a miry patch into which they had sunk. Reversing had only seemed to embed them more deeply.

'It will be okay if we can get it on to the track,' he said. 'I do not suppose you could manage the controls while I shove?' He looked at her slight figure dubiously.

'Of course I can,' she returned. 'I've driven a tractor in

124

my time.' And climbed into the driver's seat.

Inch by inch, pushing stones under the wheels and putting his shoulder against it, the machine was edged on to the comparative solidity of the track. The engine ran sweetly, and Lorena looked at him in triumph. He was breathing fast from his exertions and was streaked with dirt, his black hair hanging in elf-locks over his face. He brushed it back and grinned up her, and she was looking little better, with a smudge of oil on one cheek and her hair in wild disorder.

'That's done it!' she exclaimed, then as he made no move to join her, 'Can't we get going?'

'Get down,' he said. 'I have something to say to you first.'

'Can't it wait?' She was impatient to return, to have a wash, in hot water, and change. Her clothes had the uncomfortable feeling clothes have after being slept in.

'No, it cannot. Please, Lorena.'

Resignedly she shut off the engine, and jumped down beside him.

'Well?' she queried. 'Here I am.'

He said sententiously: 'I must in honour bound put right the situation between us. If you are a respectable young lady, you must know that you cannot spend a night alone with a man without being compromised.'

She burst out laughing. 'That's a lot of old hat,' she cried. 'It's a situation which often occurs nowadays with cars breaking down. Nobody thinks anything of it.'

'They do in Sardinia.'

'But who will know? I don't suppose Assunta or your grandmother will talk.'

'By now everyone in the village will know that you came up here and I followed you, and we spent the night alone. If they do not, Aurelio will tell them.'

'I don't mind,' she said bravely, feeling vaguely uneasy. Did he mean his grandmother would denounce her as a scarlet woman? 'When I've gone on my way, it will all be forgotten. I know and you know that nothing happened.'

'This is my country, I live here, and I am respected, a man of some influence,' he said proudly. 'I care about my reputation if you do not care about yours. It shall never be said that I brought dishonour upon a guest.'

This speech seemed to her to be absurdly old-fashioned and high-flown. Tourists abounded in Sardinia and must have brought in more advanced ideas; he had not been so squeamish when he had let Venetia suppose that they were on an unofficial honeymoon. It was only since he had begun to see her in a new light that he was having qualms of conscience. Yet his concern was wounding, almost as much as his contempt, because he was only worried about a possible scandal, irrespective of his feelings.

She looked at him uncertainly. He had donned his pullover again, and was leaning against the side of the vehicle, his arms folded, regarding her with slumbrous eyes. Again she had the impression of a beast of prey waiting to pounce.

'I don't see how any reasonable person can blame you for what didn't happen,' she said lightly. 'I assure you I don't feel in the least dishonoured. Soon I'll be gone and you can forget me. Now shall we be on our way?'

He did not move.

'When we return I shall tell *la nonna* that we are engaged,' he said calmly. 'For there is only one way out of this predicament, Lorena. I must marry you.'

In all the empty space around them, there was no human presence. The air was full of bird song and laden with the scent of flowers, butterflies flitted over thyme and thistle. It was Eden before the Fall, and what was between them was as elemental as nature's promptings to the lesser brethren all about them. But being a girl of the seventies, Lorena had to question and disbelieve the evidence of her senses, and she found Mario's pronouncement incredible. He had spoken words which she had never hoped to hear from him,

126

and he had not made them a question, but a statement; not 'will you' but 'you must'.

It was absurd, of course. In this day and age, he was under no obligation to marry her whatever, but her heart had leaped to hear him propose it, or more correctly to demand it.

Steady, she thought desperately, keep calm. Reason him out of it ... and yet ... it was a wildly impossible dream coming true. Her heart was urging her, clamouring, 'You want him. If you're honest, you must admit that you do. Accept his offer and hang the consequences.' But reason, the guiding factor which had developed throughout the centuries of man's evolution, insisted that such an idea was madness, and reason prevailed.

She essayed a shaky laugh.

'Nobody could expect you to do that.'

'Everybody will. This is no occasion for levity, Lorena.' Voice and mien were stern. 'Nobody shall throw mud at you through me.'

Of course he was thinking not of her but his own standing. She was a guest in his grandmother's house, and he feared censure from the villagers. She searched his dark, inscrutable face for some sign of emotion, but there was none. His emotions were not involved, only his sense of propriety.

She said flippantly: 'Is this anxiety about my reputation the result of discovering that I can milk a goat and drive a Land-Rover? You no longer consider I'm wholly ornamental?'

'You have shown yourself to be a young woman of resource and character, and as such I admire and respect you,' he said earnestly.

'Now you're overdoing it. It would be much more sensible to fly me out to Rome.'

He took her by her shoulders and shook her, and though there was no gentleness in his touch, she quivered under his

127

hands.

'Be serious, Lorena,' he bade her harshly. 'I refuse to run away from my responsibilities.'

'But I'm not one of them.'

'You became one when I took you to my grandmother. Perhaps that was a mistake, but it is done now.'

His hands dropped from her shoulders and he thrust them into his trouser pockets, staring over the valley beneath them with a frowning intensity. A lark soared into the sky with a burst of melody.

'Really you don't have to bother about a bit of gossip,' Lorena persisted. 'Didn't your American mother teach you a more up-to-date outlook?'

His face became bleak. 'My mother left me for *la nonna* to bring up,' he told her, 'and she is very strict in her notions.'

'I don't think I want to be married merely to placate your grandmother's prejudices,' she told him with some heat.

He made a gesture of impatience.

'You know there is more to it than that.'

'Do I?' Again she searched his face for the sign of emotion which she longed to see, but it betrayed nothing. The jaw was a little set, the eyes, still fixed on the distant horizon were unfathomable.

'You are not completely dim,' he said rudely.

'I admit I'm a little at a loss to understand your attitude at this moment,' she admitted. 'If I did take your ... er ... proposal seriously, would you expect me to give up my career?'

An expression of distaste crossed his face.

'Certainly I should. There is no necessity for my wife to work, and I would never permit her to make a spectacle of herself.'

The words 'my wife' caused her heart to miss a beat, but she said steadily:

'What if I don't want to give it up? Your views are very old-fashioned, Mario. Modern women expect to have a life of their own.'

'If by that you mean you cannot forgo attentions from other men, I shall keep you locked up,' he returned.

'I didn't mean that at all, but you are showing plainly how divergent are our views.' She drew a deep breath. 'Marriage between us would be a disaster, Mario.'

And was submerged by a wave of despair. Her reason was trying to persuade her that she spoke the truth, but her heart was still urging her to surrender.

Her words seemed to amuse him, and he turned his head to survey her with a gleam in his eyes.

'I think it would have compensations, *cara mia*.'

She turned her head away as the hot colour stained her face and neck. Physically they were drawn to each other, that she had never denied, but she suspected that sort of infatuation was transitory. He stirred and excited her, but mere sex was no foundation upon which to build a marriage. He would expect her to be submissive to his will, and though at that moment, she was ready to be so, she could not guarantee that her natural independence would not in time reassert itself. Also she would have to accept an alien mode of life in a foreign country. Only real love could stand up to such a test, and not only was she uncertain about the exact nature of her feelings for him, but she was positive that he did not love her. Physical attraction was something else altogether.

But it was very hard to give him up, although she was sure that she had no alternative. Schooling herself to speak formally, she said:

'You've done me a very great honour, and I'm touched that you're prepared to forgo your oath to marry only a Sard upon my account.' She expected him to react to that, but he remained silent and impassive. 'To marry you is quite impossible,' she concluded.

'It is not only possible but imperative,' he said shortly. 'What is the difficulty, Lorena? Although I have not got the ten thousand a year which you once said you required your husband to have ...' she hung her head at the reminder of her frivolous condition ... 'I am reasonably well off. My house in Nuoro is very different from *la nonna*'s cottage. It has all modern amenities, plus a beautiful view, and unless you are very exigent, I can give you everything you want.'

It seemed that he had not wholly ridded himself of his belief in her mercenary propensities, and she cried impulsively:

'It isn't necessary to try to buy me, Mario, but however rich you were, that would not change our different outlooks.'

'I do not doubt that we differ in many ways,' he returned. 'But we can learn to tolerate each other's points of view, though I will not permit you to continue to model.'

'There, you see. . . .' she was beginning, when she saw the flame leap in his eyes, and he interrupted fiercely:

'To hell with all this talk!' His control snapping, he swooped forward, pulling her roughly into his arms. 'I am mad for you, you little gilt-haired witch,' he muttered against her ear. 'What does anything matter except this ... and this. . . .'

Fire ran through her veins under his almost savage kisses. Doubts and fears were swamped in a delirium of the senses. She returned the pressure of his lips with abandon; her body moulded itself into his. When the storm had passed, she lay breathless and palpitating in his strict embrace, her eyes clouded by emotion.

He picked her up, and held her for a moment against his heart, which was beating as fast as her own. Then he thrust her almost roughly on to the seat of the Land-Rover.

'We must go before I lose my head completely,' he said thickly. 'There will be no more arguments, Lorena.'

She was utterly defeated. That uncomfortable reason and

common sense which had prompted her protests was completely submerged in the tides of passion which were still washing over her. Mario had used the most direct method of attack and the strongest. The womanhood which he had awakened in her accepted him as both its begetter and its master. The twentieth century was obliterated by the oldest and most primitive urges since creation. She was no longer a sophisticated modern girl with control of her destiny, but a submissive captive to her mate.

Bowing her head, she whispered: 'No, Mario.'

He went round the vehicle and climbed in beside her, starting the engine. The heavy machine lumbered down the rough track, lurching in the ruts, bumping over the stones.

They had gone some way, before she asked tentatively:

'Do you love me, Mario?'

'Have I not demonstrated that I do?'

'No. That was entirely physical—in other words, sex.'

He looked shocked at her plain speaking.

'I deplore the modern habit of analysing emotion. Such matters should not be discussed between men and maids.'

'But don't you think they should be before entering upon marriage? In Britain we believe in frank discussion of every aspect of the subject before we commit ourselves.'

He smiled wickedly. 'I think my way is more conclusive than talk, which proves nothing. I have always been told English women are cold, and I am glad that you are not an icicle, *cara mia*. Believe me, that is very important.'

She blushed. 'You took me by storm,' she accused him.

'It is the best approach,' he told her drily. 'Otherwise you would be arguing still. It worked on the boat.' Lorena blushed again. '*Dio mio*, Lorena, for one awful moment I thought that you were dead.'

'And you ... cared?'

'Do you think I am made of stone? Even if you had not been you, I would have cared, as you put it. No man would like to think that he had caused a girl's death.'

131

'But you said it was all my own fault,' she reminded him.

'Foolishness does not deserve a death penalty.'

'Ugh!' she shivered. 'But I wasn't dead. Did you really take me to your grandmother because you were afraid of my ravings?'

'Well, though I didn't want our nocturnal voyage together made public for various reasons, that was not my only motive.'

'What was the other one?'

He smiled.

'In hospital or at your friends', I should have been excluded. I wanted to keep a personal eye upon your progress towards recovery.'

'You do surprise me. From the way you scolded me when you came to the village, I should have thought you'd have been thankful to see the last of me.'

'Though I believed you to be a worthless little baggage, I was concerned for your fate. I came up every day to see how you were progressing when you were so ill. Assunta and *la nonna* wanted to cut off your beautiful hair. To pacify them I agreed to comb it every day—a penance for my obstinacy.' He looked shamefaced, as if he were confessing to a crime. 'It is so lovely, I could not bear to let them shear it.'

So it had been he who had combed her hair, the one clear impression during her delirium. The revelation moved her far more than his passionate demonstrations. As when last night he had soothed her nightmare panic, it showed a gentler side of his nature, which was more appealing than his masculine dominance.

'That was awfully sweet of you,' she said inadequately.

'There were an awful lot of tangles,' he copied her tone. 'I am afraid I often swore, *sotto voce*.'

'That I can well believe. And now you want to possess it in perpetuity? Is my hair more important than such virtues

132

as faithfulness and courage?'

'You have shown you possess courage in no small measure.'

'Don't! You overwhelm me. First you accuse me of being a mercenary bitch and now you rush to the other extreme and try to make me out a paragon.'

'You know you deliberately misled me.'

She giggled. 'I had to protect myself somehow against your irresistible charm.'

'Did you indeed? Thank you for the compliment, but I did not appreciate your methods.' He became serious. 'There is no other man in your life, Lorena? No one in England, who caused you to prevaricate?'

'There is no one, there never has been,' she assured him.

He gave a long sigh of relief. 'Forgive me,' he said almost humbly. 'I must warn you that I am a jealous man. I am glad to know that I am the first.'

But what of him? It was highly improbable that she was his first love, and wasn't he engaged? Rather belatedly she remembered Margherita Segni.

'But I'm not first with you—what about Margherita?' she enquired.

'That childish nonsense!' he exclaimed contemptuously. Lifting one hand from the steering wheel, he made a gesture as if sweeping Margherita away. 'There is no actual bond. I do not think she wants to marry me, nor does she want to spend her life in Sardinia. She will understand that where my honour is concerned, I must do what it dictates.'

That last sentence damped Lorena's rising elation, for she had begun to believe that he did love her after all. His concern over her hair, his jealousy over a possible rival had been hopeful signs, but it was the honour motive which was important to him, and the real reason for his proposal.

She said a little bitterly:

'It's lucky for you that you haven't got yourself involved with someone who is repellent to you.'

He laughed. 'But, *cara*, I would never be such a fool.'

He began to whistle cheerfully, evidently he was in high spirits, but Lorena's sank. Had she really consented to this crazy marriage, and to what had she committed herself?

He seemed to have no doubts himself, for as they neared the village, he told her:

'When we arrive I want you to go and dress yourself properly, and then we will run down to inspect my home in Nuoro, which may help to reconcile you to your fate.'

'It'll have to be very beautiful to do that,' she said archly, to which he returned simply: 'It is.'

'But what about my precious reputation?' she asked mischievously. 'Will it be correct to visit your home alone?'

'I have an elderly relative living with me who acts as my housekeeper,' he told her. 'She always acts as chaperon when Mar ... I have lady visitors.'

So he was in the habit of entertaining the Signorina Segni at his house. Uneasily she wondered if he had told her the truth about her. As if he sensed her thought, he added:

'Rita is a keen yachtswoman, we have sailed together since we were children. She often comes in for a drink after a regatta.'

Which explained everything and nothing, but before she could question further, and she was far from satisfied, he pulled up outside Lucia's house.

Lucia and Assunta were waiting in the passage beyond the front door as they entered, having heard the Land-Rover stop. Neither spoke, but their quick glances took in every detail, Lorena's wind-blown hair, her scuffed sandals and oil-smeared shirt, Mario's unshaven cheeks. Lucia's eyes were hostile and condemnatory and Lorena was assailed by a feeling of acute embarrassment. Her attitude gave point to all that Mario had been telling her, so also did Assunta's look of distress. She had been condemned unheard without the option of appeal.

Mario said harshly: 'Go upstairs and change, Lorena, while I explain what has happened, and I should prefer that you put on a skirt.'

A spurt of rebellion flared at his tone, but Lorena suppressed it, saying meekly:

'I need a wash. Could I have some hot water?'

Lucia jerked her head towards Assunta, who went to fill the brass can which was used for this purpose. She said something to Mario in dialect, while she looked as if she were about to spit, and he frowned.

'Lorena and I are to be married,' he announced stiffly.

Consternation showed in the old woman's face, while she glared at Lorena with naked animosity. Then as if a shutter had been drawn, her expression became blank.

'A drastic remedy,' she said in English. 'But I suppose a necessary one.'

Assunta returned with the can, which she thrust into Lorena's hands. She looked anxious. Lorena went upstairs with burning cheeks. She could not expect Lucia to be pleased, but she need not have shown such antagonism.

She looked like a witch about to put an evil spell upon me, she thought, and a dart of fear pierced her, as she recalled the old woman's reputation. She shrugged it off. Spells and witchcraft were all nonsense, but there was something mediaeval about the atmosphere of this place which made ill-wishing credible. She began to have some sympathy for Mario's mother. Life could not have been easy for her with Lucia for a mother-in-law.

She discarded her soiled clothes and washed all over, using the basin of warm water, while she yearned for a hot bath or a shower with scented salts, a luxury so long denied her. There was not time to wash her hair as she would have liked to do.

Arrayed in clean underwear, she rummaged through her clothes, which, in the absence of a wardrobe, were hung on hooks along one wall. Mario was already issuing his com-

135

mands, and away from him, her independence flickered, but not for long. She repressed the urge to defy his wishes by putting on a trouser suit, and selected a very feminine dress in flowered nylon, aware that in reality she wished very much to please him.

She brushed her hair until it shone and coiled it round her head. She did not hurry; she needed a little time alone to endeavour to orientate herself to her new position. She stared at her face in the square of looking glass and saw that her eyes were luminous, her mouth soft and tremulous. This was a new aspect of herself, Lorena fathoms deep in love, though reason whispered again: 'Are you sure that it is love?'

She shook her head impatiently; what was the use of splitting hairs? Mario was right, such analyses were fruitless, when her whole being yearned towards the dark inscrutable man waiting for her downstairs.

Again her reason prompted that tiresome insistence of sophistication which would not allow her to accept the dictates of her heart without question. 'He doesn't love you, all he feels for you is desire.' But that seemed to be a strong factor in his make-up, there was fire beneath that cold, proud exterior, fire which she had the power to ignite, and though it might consume her, she was ready and willing to be consumed.

'We think too much, we moderns,' she said to her image in the glass, 'and it doesn't get us anywhere. Now at last I've learned to feel.'

She completed her toilet by adding a touch of colour to her pale cheeks, and a suspicion of eye-shadow and lipstick. Outwardly she looked her usual poised sophisticated self, the blue nylon falling in soft folds about her. Inwardly she was in a fever, even after so short a while, to be with Mario again.

She went downstairs with a fast beating heart to join him.

He had shaved and his clothes had been well brushed. She saw the glow in the depths of his eyes when he saw her, and she dropped him a mocking curtsey.

'Does my appearance please my lord and master?'

'*Bella!*' he murmured. '*Bella!*'

Lucia came up to her, her face schooled to a mask, but deep in her black eyes, malevolence still lurked.

'So we are to welcome you into the family,' she said coldly.

'Well, yes, I suppose so,' Lorena rejoined awkwardly, thinking welcome was hardly the operative word. She suspected that Lucia would rather see her dead than married to Mario, but she was after all only a prejudiced old woman.

Assunta to her relief was looking pleased.

'I am very glad,' she said, and came up to her to kiss her. 'It is worth the anxiety over Gigi for this to happen.'

'Gigi is all right?'

'*Si*, Nonna send him next door to play,' Assunta told her uncomfortably.

So my wicked presence would not contaminate him, Lorena thought shrewdly. Assunta went on:

'I owe you a thousand thanks, Lorena, but your long walk lead you to love.' She looked coyly at her cousin.

'Love!' Lucia exclaimed harshly. 'The most ephemeral thing in the world. Love did not save your mother's marriage, Mario.'

A slight shadow crossed the man's face, and for a moment he looked disconcerted. Then he laughed.

'Be done with your croaking, Nonna,' he told her. 'We cannot all be unlucky.' He held out his hand to Lorena. 'Come,' he bade her.

She laid hers in it, feeling it was an act of surrender. He led her out of the house, and she saw the Land-Rover had gone and his car stood in its place. He opened the door for her, and she got in, thankful to leave Lucia's oppressive

137

presence.

Assunta stood in the doorway, waving to them and smiling.

'*Addio, e presto ritorno,*' she called.

A return which Lorena supposed was inevitable. Was she expected to go on living with Lucia until ...? Then as Mario took his place beside her, a surge of triumph washed over her. In spite of Lucia, Margherita and his vow to marry only one of his countrywomen, she had won this proud, haughty Sard, and what was between them could by patience and understanding be converted into lasting love. Sardinia had given her something which she had never expected to experience, a deep and overwhelming passion for a man.

Doubts and misgivings cast aside, her spirits rocketed as Mario negotiated the steep, winding road down to Nuoro.

CHAPTER SEVEN

THE town of Nuoro sprawled along a ridge at a height of eighteen thousand feet above sea level, and was divided from the surrounding mountains by wide valleys. Monte Oliena, a bleached dolomite mass, lifted a jagged crest to the sky in the south, while the slopes of Monte Ortobene rose behind it.

Building here, as elsewhere, was in progress in the form of square blocks of flats and offices, mainly on the outskirts of the town. In the centre, a long thoroughfare intersected a maze of old alleyways. The main square was filled with stalls and kiosks, and, as in every Sardo town, barbers' shops, bars and tobacconists predominated among stores selling refrigerators, television sets and the latest fashion wear, innovations which showed that the country moved with the times.

After her seclusion in the village, Lorena felt as if she were returning to civilised life after a long stay in the backwoods. She was childishly delighted to see some real shops again, and Mario viewed her enthusiasm indulgently.

'I fear country life has no great appeal for you,' he remarked.

'There's country and country,' she pointed out. 'You must admit last night was rather excessively rural,' and flushed as she caught his mocking glance. Perhaps the previous night was a subject best avoided.

Mario's house was situated a further fifteen thousand feet up, nearly at the top of Monte Ortobene. The spiralling road to it was lined with oleanders, broom, lilac and blackberry blossom, backed by fig trees, pines and ilex. There was a hotel and a small public garden, surrounded by several *ristorantes* and private villas on this ledge of the

139

mountain. At the very summit was a bronze statue of the Redeemer, served by a stone altar, which was a focal point for pilgrimages, Mario told her. On the twenty-ninth of August, a great procession came up from Nuoro, led by the bishop and priests, followed by, first the choir, and then a host of men and women all wearing their beautiful regional costumes. A service of thanksgiving was held, after which singing, dancing and merrymaking were carried on until midnight.

'Once it was a genuine pilgrimage,' he said regretfully, 'but nowadays it is degenerating into a mere tourist attraction. All the same it is worth seeing, if only for the dresses, and you will be a spectator this year, of course.'

Lorena acquiesced meekly, though she did not feel his certainty. August was still some way off.

His own house was below the mountain summit, a white building with a flat roof, surrounded by a high wall on three sides. Wrought iron gates led into a paved courtyard. Mario drove through the gates which were set ajar, and a lithe young Sard came running to close them behind the car.

'Take it round to the garage,' Mario told him as he got out. 'I shall not be needing it again until late afternoon.'

He came to Lorena's door and handed her out as if she had been a duchess, while the boy made an obeisance to her, his dark eyes full of wonder as if he had seen a vision. Then he glanced at his master and his look of awe changed to a significant grin.

'This lady is to be your mistress, Stefano,' Mario told him curtly, noticing his knowing look. 'She will live here after our marriage.'

Stefano looked startled at this revelation, and he eyed Lorena with new respect. Mario drew her hand through his arm and led her towards the house.

The imposing entrance door was also open, and they passed through into the cool dimness of a spacious hall, at the further end of which doors opened on to a terrace, framing a glowing picture of sunlight shining on white marble and potted plants.

A woman came hurrying to greet them. She was unfashionably dressed in a black blouse and long skirt, with her scanty grey hair drawn back into a bun. She had black eyes set in an oval face and the malarial skin of her generation, for before the marshes had been cleared of the malaria mosquito, that disease had been a scourge throughout the country. Mario introduced her as Paulina Ferri.

She politely wished them good day, adding reproachfully:

'We expected you last night, Mario. The dinner which I had prepared with my own hands was wasted.'

Mario expressed his regret for his non-appearance, saying he had been unavoidably detained. He was careful not to look at Lorena, who stifled a desire to giggle. Instead of a no doubt delectable meal, Mario had had to content himself with a shepherds' stew, and it had all been upon her account. He went on to tell Paulina that he hoped she would prepare for them an equally appetising lunch, of which she must partake with them. A gleam came into her eyes.

'In the capacity of a chaperon for the *signorina*,' she suggested demurely, understanding him perfectly.

'Precisely. Meanwhile perhaps one of the girls will be so good as to bring us coffee on to the terrace.'

'But of course.' She hurried away and Lorena was left with the uncomfortable impression that this was not the first time that she had acted as chaperon to Mario's lady guests. But she forgot all about it as she stepped outside.

The marble paved terrace was furnished with brightly coloured chairs and loungers and beyond the balustrade was a view ... and what a view! She ran eagerly to lean over to look at it. Mountains and valleys were spread out before her, the pale mass of craggy Oliena standing out from the darker wooded hills around it. On the far horizon, the bulk

141

of the Gennargentu massif loomed, blue layers fading to a misty nothingness. Due east, a faint line indicated the sea. In the foreground, a terraced garden descended the hill side, massed with flowers, with butterflies flitting from bloom to bloom. The scent of sage, rosemary and thyme filled the air with aromatic fragrance.

'What a heavenly place, Mario!' she exclaimed.

He came up beside her, laying a possessive arm across her shoulders, and her pulses quickened at the gesture.

'I was sure you would like it, and it is a fitting setting for you, my love,' he said softly. 'This is to be your home.'

Involuntarily she recalled the high walls behind her, the forbidding gateway, shutting out the world, and his threat to lock her up, if she allowed her fancy to stray.

'Is this where you keep your seraglio?' she asked lightly.

'You will find no houris here. This is where I shall house my bride.'

He stooped and kissed her quickly, then drew away as if he did not trust himself to be too near to her.

'Paulina will prepare a real Sardo lunch for us,' he went on. 'I hope you will enjoy it.'

'You said she was a relative, didn't you?' Lorena asked, having noted that she addressed her master by his name.

'Yes. She is a family connection who was left in poor circumstances. I installed her here and she looks after me like a second mother.' He gave a quick sigh and Lorena guessed that he had never ceased to regret his real mother's desertion.

'I hope she won't resent me,' she said doubtfully, for Paulina's direct assessing gaze had not been friendly.

He smiled ironically. 'Why should she? She knows that I must marry and bring a mistress here, and you will be easier than ... some others might be.'

'Must?' she queried. 'Are you under some compulsion to wed?'

He looked at her sombrely. 'I am the last of our line, now

Guido has gone. It is my duty to marry. I am lucky that duty and inclination go hand in hand. Now if you will excuse me I will go and make myself presentable to match your elegance. Coffee will not be long. In the meantime——' he took an album from a shelf in the corner, 'perhaps it would amuse you to look at this. I used to fancy myself as a photographer.'

Lorena took the book from him, and left alone, sat down, opening it upon her knee. She leafed through it idly. It contained views of the island, some of which she recognised, including dramatic rock formations in the Gallura area, pictures of interesting buildings, one of Lucia sitting in her garden, and another of Assunta in regional dress, the long skirt with embroidered hem, velvet bodice and lawn sleeves. It seemed odd to connect Mario with photography, yet why not? It brought home to her how little she knew about him. The last pages were of more personal interest. They were covered with snapshots of two dark-haired teenage boys and a girl. They were all taken by the sea and a sailing dinghy figured in most of them. The two boys were recognisable as Mario and Guido, and she studied them eagerly. The girl was not Assunta, though obviously Sardo; Assunta must have been a child at the time these were taken. She was evidently familiar with boats; there was one of her hoisting the mainsail. There was another of her with Mario's arm across her shoulders. Both were laughing. Lorena suspected that she was Margherita.

Paulina herself brought out the coffee. She set the tray down on a low Turkish table of carved wood inlaid with mother of pearl.

'Mario will prefer a whisky, so there will be no need to wait for him,' she said, and proceeded to pour it out.

She noticed the book on Lorena's knee, open at the page of snapshots.

'Those are the Marescu boys, of course,' she told her. 'With Rita. They spent all their holidays together afloat.'

143

She sighed. 'Poor Rita!'

'The Signorina Segni?' Lorena asked, closing the book.

'*Si*. She and Mario were childhood sweethearts.'

This statement seemed to suggest a greater degree of intimacy between the couple than that which Mario had admitted, and Paulina was apparently on Margherita's side, for there was a hint of reproach in her eyes.

Lorena said carefully: 'Such connections often fade out when young people grow older. Does he see much of her now?'

'She is away in Italy a good deal, but we have regattas at which they meet. Both are still keen sailors. Do you care for that sport, *signorina*?'

'I haven't done much,' Lorena admitted, with a lively recollection of her last experience at sea, which had hardly been pleasant.

'Doubtless Mario will teach you,' Paulina observed, looking at her as if she considered she was a most unlikely candidate for such instruction. 'Have you known him long?'

She handed Lorena her coffee cup, which she noticed was of fine china. All Mario's appointments were the best of their kind, and she remembered that he had said he liked to have beautiful things about him.

'Not very long,' she admitted, fearing she was going to be put through a catechism about her association with Mario, which would be difficult to parry, but though Paulina's mind was obviously seething with questions, she confined herself to enquiring:

'You like our country?'

Lorena assured her that she admired all things Sardi, while Paulina nodded her head and her lips curled in a little contemptuous smile.

'You see it with a visitor's eyes, *signorina*, but it will be very different when you become a native,' she said warningly. 'You may not find it easy to be a good wife to Mario.'

'I don't suppose I shall, but I will do my best.'

'Your best may not be good enough. Great tact and discretion will be required in your position and an understanding of the people if you are not to show yourself the reed that breaks.'

Lorena moved uneasily, slightly puzzled by this ambiguous statement. What was Mario's position and what part had she in his activities? She longed to ask outright what they were, but loyalty restrained her, nor did she want to betray to this unsympathetic woman that there had not been time for him to confide in her.

'His friends will be greatly surprised,' Paulina went on, 'It has always been expected he would marry a Sard. In fact it is almost obligatory.'

'A man has a right to choose whom he wants to marry,' Lorena said drily, 'without consulting his friends' opinion.'

'A man can be blinded by infatuation,' Paulina suggested slyly.

'Oh, really!' Lorena exclaimed impatiently.

At that point, to her relief, Mario returned. He had changed into a light suit which showed the hand of a good tailor, and was immaculate down to the silk handkerchief in his breast pocket.

After pouring for him the whisky which, as she had said, he preferred at that hour, Paulina withdrew to prepare their meal, and Mario relaxed in a chair beside Lorena, stretching out his long, grey-trousered legs to the caress of the sun.

He began to talk lazily about the country, describing its turbulent history. He told her how Garibaldi had lived on an island in the north, and died there. One day he would take her to see his house and statue, the former being left exactly as it had been as a memorial to the hero. Lord Nelson had visited the island and had advised his government to annex it if possible, because of its excellent harbours.

'But his enthusiasm evoked no response, and that is the

145

nearest we ever came to being British,' he said, laughing.

Lorena listened to him with interest, though she would have preferred a more intimate topic of conversation. Mario presented so many contradictions, and she was still groping for a fuller understanding of him.

Lunch was served in the airy dining room decorated in white and green with a shining parquet floor. Paulina sat upon one side of Mario, at the head of the table, Lorena on the other.

She had provided Sardinian smoked ham, *porchetto*— sucking pig—with salad and a dessert of cherries and peaches, the latter being the finest Lorena had ever seen. They drank the red wine of the country.

Upon one wall was a mural depicting Persephone in the Underworld, accepting the half of a pomegranate from her dark-visaged lord, the fatal fruit which meant that she must always return to him. Mario explained that the fresco had been rescued from the ruins of a Roman villa, for the Romans in their time had left their mark upon the island. Lorena thought that she could trace in the lineaments of the King of Hades a faint resemblance to Mario. As if guessing the trend of her thoughts, he startled her by saying:

'Persephone was returned to her sorrowing mother, but because she had eaten in the underworld, she had to return thither for part of the year. You, my nymph, have eaten rather more than a few pomegranate seeds,' he glanced at the remains of roast pig, 'so we can take it you will leave me never.'

'When is the wedding going to be?' Paulina intervened.

'As soon as possible,' Mario returned. 'I will see about the formalities right away.'

'Don't I have any say in the matter?' Lorena asked. 'I would like to go home first and see my people.'

'We will both go—later on.' He looked at her meaningfully. 'There is every reason for urgency.'

Lorena saw the question in Paulina's eyes, and hastened

146

to explain.

'Owing to an unfortunate accident Mario fears gossip,' she said, hating to have to make the admission, especially as she saw an expression of enlightenment dawn on the woman's face.

'Ah!' she exclaimed. 'So that is it.'

'Is what?' Mario asked sharply, but Paulina merely shrugged.

He changed the subject, asking her some commonplace questions about the running of the house, to which she responded with a voluble flood of Italian.

Lorena toyed with a peach and glanced surreptitiously at the classic profile of the Lord of the Underworld upon the wall, which was so similar to that of the man seated next to her. His insistence upon an early marriage and the reason for it had hurt her. Could he really be so scared by tittle-tattle? It was her right to be married from her own home, not in some hole-and-corner place in a foreign land. She would have more to say about that when she was alone with him.

But when they were back upon the terrace, and more coffee was brought to them, she found she was unwilling to raise the subject. A pleasant languor had descended upon her. After her poor night and early rising, her surroundings were beginning to take on a dream-like quality. She had entered a faerie world, and the awakening, if awakening there must be would come soon enough.

She lay full length on a canvas chaise-longue, completely relaxed, while Mario lounged beside her smoking a cigar. Elegantly dressed, his smooth olive face inscrutable, he watched her possessively. Surrounded by delightful scents and scenery, she surrendered to a mood of voluptuous contentment. For this one day at least she would cease to probe and ponder and give herself up to sheer enjoyment of the moment and the presence of this fascinating personality, who, unbelievably, had asked her to marry him.

147

Presently he said: 'You look half asleep. Perhaps you would like to have a siesta while I perform a small errand which I want to do before I take you back to the village. I wish I did not have to do that, but I cannot keep you here without benefit of clergy.' He smiled mischievously. 'You must not try to keep me waiting, *carina mia*, lest I become too impatient.'

He stood up, and stretched his arms above his head. A whiff of lavender and old spice reached her. He had, when he went to change enjoyed a quick bath or a shower, and she had a sudden longing to immerse herself in hot water, so much more satisfying than the sponge down which was all she could achieve in Lucia's house. She said tentatively:

'I wonder ... if instead of a siesta, you would think me awful if I had a bath while you're gone? I haven't had a proper tub for ages.'

He looked slightly taken aback, then he laughed.

'I know my grandmother's house lacks mod cons, and after a night in that hut, I can understand your feelings, though you look perfectly clean. I will go and ask Paulina to run one for you.'

'Oh, please don't bother her,' Lorena said quickly, feeling sure the housekeeper would disapprove of such unconventionality. 'Just show me where the bathroom is and I can manage.'

'Come along, then.'

She had of course been shown the cloakroom, but that was situated elsewhere. The bathroom was tiled in green and like the one at the Riccis' surrounded by mirrors. A wet splodge on the bath mat and marks made by steam running down the mirrors indicated that the room had had a recent tenant. Mario's shaving tackle was laid out on a shelf, and a dark robe hung on the door.

Mario glanced round disparagingly. 'The maid has not been in to clear up after me.'

'It doesn't matter, hot water is the main thing.'

She sensed he was embarrassed and felt so herself. He looked at her with an odd expression, and she felt the tension in him.

'You will find clean towels in that cupboard,' he told her. He stooped as if to kiss her, then checked himself abruptly. *'Ciao, carina,'* he said casually, and hurried away with obvious relief.

Lorena was momentarily chilled by his withdrawal, for it had been a definite withdrawal. Did he feel that she had claimed an intimacy which was premature? But if they were to be married soon, what did it signify? His views, she thought were a strange mingling of prudishness and licence, and perhaps she would have been wiser not to have made her request.

Then she forgot all about her qualms in the sheer pleasure of hot water and scented bath salts, of which a tall jar stood on a shelf. She became aware that the soap she was using was his, he had used it too. When she got out of the bath, she carefully set her foot in the place where his had damped the mat. Since he was not there she could give full rein to her delight in being where he had been, touching what he had touched. The mirrors which reflected her body had reflected his a short while previously. She closed her eyes and imagined his lean brown strength beside her, then blushed at her sensuous thoughts.

She dressed herself, but when it came to putting up her hair, she hesitated. Since they would be alone together, she would leave it loose, as it seemed to give him so much pleasure, and Paulina could think what she chose. She combed it, remembering he had told her that he had performed that office for her during her illness. Was that really true, she wondered, or merely a pretty story concocted to please her? It seemed such an unlikely attention.

Her hands were roughened and reddened by the hard usage of the previous night and morning. She could do nothing about them, but at least they bore witness that she

149

could be useful as well as ornamental. Then shaking her hair over her shoulders, she went blithely back to the terrace.

At first she thought Mario had already returned, when she glimpsed a dark head above the back of a lounger chair, but when its occupant stood up at her approach, she saw it was a woman. The newcomer had aquiline features and a bush of black hair cut short. She was not tall, but her figure was slim and elegant. She wore navy slacks and a nautically styled jacket, blue with gilt buttons and trimmed with white braid. She appeared to be in her late twenties, or even thirty, and possessed a hard, polished assurance, which made Lorena in her girlish dress with her hair flowing down her back feel juvenile and vulnerable, and very much at a disadvantage.

Her visitor looked her up and down with a quizzical look that was not unlike Mario's.

'Very pretty,' she said. 'What a pity Mario isn't here to admire. I'm afraid he won't be along yet awhile. He's discussing boats with my father, and once they get together on that subject, there's no dislodging them.'

Her English was accentless and idiomatic.

'Did he send you to tell me that?' Lorena faltered, thinking with dismay that if Mario had become bored with her society without the diversion of lovemaking after only a few hours, it boded ill for their marriage.

'I'm no man's messenger,' the other said haughtily. 'Paulina rang me up to tell me you were here. She thought we ought to meet, so when I found the gentleman we're both interested in was otherwise employed, I came along to have a look at you. It's always good strategy to view the enemy's strong points at close quarters.'

'I think there's been a misunderstanding,' Lorena returned, wishing that she had put her hair up, for the other girl was eyeing it with amused speculation. 'I wasn't aware that you were my enemy.'

'What else? Haven't you stolen my man?'

So this must be Margherita Segni, and far from accepting Mario's airy dismissal of their engagement, she had come to assert her rights.

'Not intentionally,' Lorena told her coolly. 'I suppose you are the Signorina Segni?'

'So you have heard of me?'

'Yes, *signorina*, and may I point out that a man can't be stolen without his consent. Mario gave me to understand that you were no longer interested in him.'

'Oh, he did, did he? Then may *I* point out that a man will make all sorts of misrepresentations when he's in the throes of a mad infatuation, for that is what it is, of course. Surely you're not so naïve as to imagine it'll last?'

This being what Lorena herself feared, she was not grateful to her visitor for putting her doubts into words.

'Suppose we sit down?' Margherita went on suavely. 'No need for you to stand at bay like that.' She perched herself on the top of the balustrade, with complete assurance, and Lorena subsided into a chair.

'I like this house,' Margherita observed. 'Nice situation, don't you think?' She was looking about her appreciatively.

'Beautiful,' Lorena murmured, feeling she was confronting an unpredictable cat who at any minute would unsheath its claws.

Margherita's gaze fastened upon Lorena, and she surveyed her from top to toe appraisingly.

'I must admit you're very pretty,' she said, 'so there's some excuse for him. You're a mannequin, aren't you?'

Lorena stared. 'How on earth did you know that?'

'I'm just back from Rome, where I'm acquainted with Venetia Manners.'

'What a coincidence!'

'Not at all. Venetia works for the best couturier in that city and I shop there. It was she who put me wise to what was going on here. She seemed to think you needed to be

151

rescued from a crazy entanglement.'

'She's under a misapprehension.' Lorena was secretly cursing Venetia's indiscreet tongue. She had never forgiven her for not accepting Giulio, and Mario had let her imagine a situation which did not exist, with this unlucky consequence.

'So it seems,' Margherita concurred. 'Paulina says he's going to marry you. I must say it was quite a shock to discover you'd managed to hook him.'

Lorena winced at the crude expression, which sounded incongruous on this proud-looking girl's lips.

'Your English is very colloquial,' she remarked curiously.

'Learnt it at one of your English schools where I was for some years. Posh place it was too, though the girls were all morons. Always sighing for romance when they weren't playing games. I showed them Mario's photograph and told them he was my fiancé. They thought he was—what was the expression?—a dreamboat.'

This information was unpalatable to Lorena, betraying as it did that Margherita's engagement had been an understood thing for a long time. Mario had misled her about his true relationship with the girl. It did explain Paulina's hostility. She thought that Margherita had been jilted in a particularly heartless manner.

'Of course that's a long time ago,' Margherita admitted. 'I'm not so soppy now. I'm studying art in Rome, and learning the ways of the world.' She put one foot upon the balustrade and clasped her knee, while she continued to contemplate Lorena out of sloe-black, narrowed eyes. 'Venetia says your name is Lorena—is that a fact, or only a *nom de guerre*? Sounds a bit mushy to me.'

'It is actually my name,' Lorena returned, rather puzzled by the girl's inconsequent talk. 'My intimate friends call me Rena.'

'And mine call me Rita. Rena and Rita, sounds like a variety turn.' She laughed gaily, then said more seriously,

'And Mario is the third member of the trio. One of us, my dear, is the other woman, the question is—which? I consider I have the prior claim, but you seem to be in possession. The odds I think are even. I wonder what made you latch on to him. Was it his income that attracted you—this house—or his position?'

Lorena saw Venetia's influence behind this question.

'None of that,' she said indignantly, 'it was Mario himself ...' She broke off. Why should she confess her feelings to this insolent woman, who would pour scorn upon them?

'Mario himself,' Margherita mimicked her. 'How touching! So you fell for his *beaux yeux*? He looks very nice—outside, but what do you really know about him?'

'I'm learning quite a lot,' Lorena retorted. The question was only too pertinent, but to answer it truthfully would betray too much. She ought to be resenting this catechism, but there was a straightforwardness, almost friendliness about the Sard's manner which was difficult to resist.

'I bet you don't know him at all,' Margherita proclaimed. 'He has all the best and worst traits of our race, overlaid by a modern education plus a chip on his shoulder with regard to his mother. I understand him, but I doubt if you ever will. He's impatient, even harsh with those who oppose him, but he is capable of great tenderness towards the weak and ailing. I remember once when I hurt my ankle ...' Her voice trailed away, and the hard face softened as she looked towards Oliena's slopes.

Lorena felt a sharp stab of jealousy; she also knew how tender Mario could be with those in distress. That Margherita had also been a recipient of it was unwelcome news, though it was only to be expected.

Margherita brought her gaze back to her. 'That was also a long time ago,' she confessed. 'Has he told you about his ambitions?'

'No,' Lorena admitted reluctantly. He had hardly had time.

'Then I will put you in the picture. This year he will be elected mayor of the province. His ultimate goal is a seat in the Senate as representative for Sardinia. He might, when he is old enough, even be made a senator.'

Lorena knew very little about the administration of the country; vaguely she was aware that it was autonomous, though officially under Italian jurisdiction.

'To represent his country in the Senate will be a great honour,' Margherita went on, 'but he needs a wife who will be a help to him, and obviously she should be a Sard.'

So that was what Paulina's hints had meant to convey. Lorena was overwhelmed by a sense of her own inadequacy; she knew nothing whatever about politics.

'Moreover he wants children,' Margherita continued, and now she put out her claws. 'I imagine he is captivated by your extreme fairness, that hair—it is a web in which to entangle a man's dreams. His mother was also alien, but dark as a gypsy, no problem there, but I doubt he'll want to see your colouring reproduced in his sons, as it might be. A tow-haired brood of little Marescus would be embarrassing to one who has dedicated his life to the service of the true Sards.'

'I suppose he has considered all that,' Lorena said faintly, but she did not believe he had. The quip about the tow-haired brood had been subtly wounding, as was intended.

'Not him!' Margherita declared rudely. 'He's been carried away by his infatuation.' She laughed a little cruelly. 'An ex-model as his lady mayoress!'

Goaded beyond discretion, Lorena blurted out:

'It's Mario who insists upon marrying me, not I him. I told him it wouldn't work. He believes he has compromised me.'

'Ah, he fears a slur upon his public image,' Margherita looked pleased. 'So that's all it is. Of course he can't afford a scandal.' She looked at Lorena consideringly. 'Does he have to make an honest woman of you? Venetia said he

154

went away with you, but I couldn't believe he'd do such a thing.'

'No!' Lorena exclaimed vehemently. 'It wasn't like that at all. We were caught in a fog, nothing happened, but ...' Recalling what had finally clinched the argument, she felt herself blush. 'He said it was a matter of honour and you would understand,' she finished lamely.

Margherita laughed contemptuously. 'Mario and his honour! It's always been a bit of a fetish with him. He must be in a bit of a dilemma now, dishonour either way, me jilted or you compromised, but I think I know what clinched his decision.' She pointed to Lorena's hair. 'Do you tint it?' she asked.

'No, of course not,' Lorena brushed aside the unimportant question. She realised that Mario had not had a chance to see the Sardo girl and make his explanations. That Margherita had learned of his infidelity through a third party was unfortunate, if he had been unfaithful. She said doubtfully:

'Then you are officially engaged to him?' for she had seen no ring on Margherita's brown rather stubby fingers.

'It was arranged in our cradles in the good old island way,' Margherita announced.

'I've never thought arranged marriages could be very happy ones,' Lorena suggested diffidently. She looked the Sardo girl straight in the face. 'Tell me truthfully, do you love Mario?'

For that would be the decisive factor. Dubious about Mario's real feelings for herself, she could not deprive Margherita of her lover—if they were lovers.

Margherita laughed. 'Oh, come off it, Rena! I'm rather past romantic yearnings; Mario and I have a good relationship, we are friends, we like the same things, we agree upon every subject but one, we have similar backgrounds and we are the same nationality. A good foundation for marriage, don't you think?'

Lorena said nothing; there was one thing missing, but

155

that Margherita did not seem to think important. She herself possessed none of the foundation stones mentioned, but she did love. If only she knew if her love was returned!

Margherita was watching her pensive face shrewdly.

'I hope for your sake you're planning a long engagement,' she suggested. 'Then there will be time for you both to reconsider your folly.'

Lorena still did not speak, but she looked conscious and Margherita exclaimed:

'You're not? Then something will have to be done about it. You don't imagine I'll tamely surrender him to you?'

'Isn't it for Mario to decide?' Lorena asked.

'No, it's up to you. I'm paying you the compliment of believing you're a sensible young woman. You said yourself you didn't think it would work, and you wouldn't wilfully trespass, would you?'

'No, but the knowledge that I'm trespassing has come rather late in the day,' Lorena returned. 'If I were convinced Mario's happiness lay with you ...' She broke off and considered the other girl. She had a hard face, she thought, and an arrogant air; she would not be a submissive wife.

'Upon what subject do you disagree?' she asked.

'It's not important and I'm sure I can bring him round to my way of thinking,' Margherita said evasively. 'That is if I'm given a free hand. I gather that in spite of all I've told you, you intend to cling to him? You're besotted, aren't you? Don't you think he may come to find you a bit cloying?'

Her latent jealousy, so well disguised until now, showed in her so dark eyes, and an acid note had crept into her voice.

'I ... I shall have to talk to Mario about the points you've raised,' Lorena told her. 'I think he owes me some explanations.'

'But you won't get them,' Margherita said viciously. 'That man is as devious as they come. But when he recovers

156

from his madness, and finds himself tied to you, he'll bitterly regret the mess he's made of his life, and so will you, when this love you set such store by begins to cool. But I'll fight you tooth and nail to stop it, before it's too late!'

Her hitherto urbane manner slipped from her. Her lips curled back from her white teeth, while her eyes shone red, betraying that she had her full share of her people's violent nature.

'You'd like to stick a knife into me, wouldn't you?' Lorena observed.

Margherita drew a long breath and recovered her poise. 'Nothing so crude,' she returned. 'I'm more subtle than that. I can't compete with you physically, but there are other methods.' She slipped off the balustrade. 'I'd better be going. Mario may be coming back at long last, and it wouldn't be good tactics to let him find me here.'

She put her hands on her hips and regarded Lorena insolently.

'I'm sorry you won't be sensible,' she said. 'Under other circumstances, I could have liked you. Think over all I've said, and I hope for your own sake you'll have second thoughts. Don't mention that you've seen me, for if you use any of the arguments I've outlined, they will be more effective if Mario believes you've thought of them yourself.'

'Thank you for your advice,' Lorena returned, an angry spot of colour on either cheek. 'I will certainly think over what you've said, but I reiterate, the choice between us lies with Mario.'

'Then he must be induced to think again too,' Margherita retorted. 'Remember, I hold him by ties of long association and you're just a flash in the pan.'

She walked across the terrace, turning back to add:

'Possibly you'll run into me again and soon, but I shan't let on that we've already met. That would entail too many explanations, as I'm sure you'll agree. *Arrivederci*, Rena.'

She was gone, like the passing of a dark cloud over the sunlit terrace. Lorena got up and went to the balustrade, her eyes seeking the distant hills.

'I will lift up mine eyes unto the hills from whence comes my help.'

She needed help and strength for the interview with Margherita had shattered her serenity, shaken her confidence, she felt lost and uncertain what course to pursue. Hitherto the Sardo girl had been a somewhat vague image, but now she had materialised into a hard and uncompromising fact, and so much of what she had said had made sense. She, Lorena, had had no idea of Mario's civic aspirations, though she knew he was considered to be an influential man. She could understand how a breath of scandal could ruin his career. Marrying her would scotch any risk of that, but she had always thought it would be a simpler remedy for her to disappear. People had short memories and apart from the Costa Smeralda, nobody knew of her existence, except the villagers.

But Mario had said there was more to it than that and had overwhelmed her objections with his kisses. He was, as he had said, linking necessity with inclination, but she suspected that if the emergency had not arisen he would never have dreamed of marrying her. Although he desired her with all the force of his turbulent nature, he would have sent her away. Circumstances, however, had changed and overridden his discretion.

He was not looking beyond the present, but the fires which she had lit would burn fast and furiously leaving only grey ash, and when his passion was slaked, what then? He would discover she was inadequate as a public man's wife, and remember how well Margherita would have filled the position; his colleagues would look askance at his ill-chosen mate, his children would remind him of her foreign origin, for what had hurt her most was Margherita's scornful reference to the possibility of tow-headed Marescus. A small thing perhaps amid the wider issues, but possibly far-reaching. Proud of his own heritage, fiercely patriotic as he was, their colouring could be a perpetual reminder to him of the folly he had committed when he had insisted upon their union.

For her own part, she would be utterly dependent upon his companionship and affection in a country where she had no friend. Even Assunta would be going back to Rome, and if he failed her, she would be lost. Could she risk it?

Margherita had also said that it was up to her to disentangle the threads of their joint destinies, and loving him desperately it would take more strength than she possessed to leave him.

Her head and eyes ached, the glare of the sunlight hurt them. The enchantment had gone from her surroundings; the cicadas kept up a maddening chorus, the heavy scent from the flowers in the garden was cloying in its sweetness. Cloying? Margherita chose her words well. Would her love for Mario become that? Was not he even now discussing yachts with Signor Segni, having found her company tedious?

What was she going to do? Tell him she had seen Margherita? Upbraid him for jilting her? Reiterate all the old arguments? His reaction was predictable. He would brush her protests aside, insist his honour was more important than his fiancée's claims, and she would again succumb.

She decided she would say nothing, but when she had returned to the village, in the solitude of her own room, away from the overpowering influence of his presence, she would think—think hard and pray to be able to arrive at the right decision.

She heard his voice in the hall, speaking to Paulina, and her heart seemed to stop, and then start beating again in double time. She must not let him sense her inner disturbance, he was very quick to catch her moods.

Drawing a deep breath to steady herself, she turned round to greet him.

CHAPTER EIGHT

MARIO came light-footed on to the terrace, and beholding him, Lorena's doubts and fears dissolved as dew before the rays of the sun. The love light came into her eyes, delicate colour rose in her cheeks, and her lips became tremulous. Her hair rippled over her shoulders, a metallic flood of silver and gold.

He stopped abruptly and paled. There was no response in his face, it was marble hard and cold, while his eyes were jetty stones. He said harshly:

'*Dio mio*, Lorena, are you mad? Put up that hair!'

She wilted under his displeasure, and he added more gently: 'You will shock Paulina, and someone might call.'

Someone had called; she wondered if Paulina had told him of Margherita's visit and that was what had changed him. Dispiritedly she looked round for a mirror, and seeing none, said:

'I shall have to go back to the bathroom to do it.'

'Please go at once.' It was a command.

Reluctantly she went, amazed at the fuss he was making. After all, he had often seen her with her hair loose, though not in conjunction with a becoming dress. Carelessly she twisted it up around her head, not caring what it looked like. Her innocent little effort to please him had gone sadly awry. The joyous mood in which she had come from her bath had fled beyond recall—was it only a short while ago? What had Signor Segni said to put Mario in such a filthy mood? Perhaps he had been interceding upon his daughter's behalf? She rejoined him, saying resentfully:

'Will that do?'

He was standing by the balustrade smoking, constraint in every line of him, and he barely glanced at her.

'Thank you, yes,' he said briefly. 'Did you enjoy your bath?'

He made the question sound as if she had been guilty of a misdemeanour.

'Yes, very much,' she replied mechanically.

He seemed distrait, and kept giving her quick glances and turning away. All the pleasant intimacy that had been between them earlier in the day had vanished.

'You were gone a long time,' she said reproachfully.

'I ran into an old friend,' he told her shortly. 'I expected you would be some time and there was no need to hurry.'

Definitely Signor Segni had said something to upset him.

'I think it must be time I went back,' she said desperately. She could not stand much more of this. He had become a not very polite stranger.

He glanced at his watch. 'Wouldn't you like some tea or something?' he asked vaguely.

'No, thank you.'

He stubbed out his cigarette. 'I have been thinking that you might be more comfortable staying at a hotel until our wedding,' he suggested. 'There are plenty of suitable places here. Would you like that?'

'I think I'd prefer to stay on in the village,' she told him. 'I'm used to it now and I'm fond of Assunta and Gigi.'

She would be further away from him there if she decided to escape from this situation which had never been quite real and was rapidly becoming more impossible every minute.

He put his hand in his pocket and drew out a small case.

'I went to fetch this from the bank,' he told her. He snapped it open to disclose a ring in which a great emerald was set in gold. 'The Marescu betrothal ring,' he said absently, moving it to and fro so that the light struck green fire from the stone. 'My mother left it behind when she went, and it will have to be cleaned, but I want to see how it fits for size.'

'You mean I'm to wear it?' Lorena faltered.

'But of course.' He held it out to her. 'Put it on.'

She obeyed, thinking he ought to have put it on for her, but he seemed to shrink from contact with her. It felt heavy and insecure on her finger.

'Yes, it is too big,' he said. 'We must ascertain the correct measurement,' and looked about for something to use as a gauge.

'There's no hurry, is there?' she asked, thinking that Margherita's hands had appeared to be bigger than hers, and the ring would not have to be altered if. ... It was rather strange that he had not already given it to the Sardo girl, if ... another if. ... She slipped the ring off and saw there was an inscription inside it.

'What does it say?' she asked, trying to decipher the tiny lettering.

'*Omnia vincit amor*,' he said softly.

Love conquers all things; if only Mario loved her, she would have no fears for the future, Margherita's claims notwithstanding. Love could smooth away the most unsurmountable obstacles. Mario would accept fair-haired children gladly if he loved her, because they would be hers. He would be patient with her social blunders, he would forgive her alien birth, if he loved her, but did he?

He took the ring from her, turning it in his fingers, and she looked at him searchingly, intensely aware of his good looks, his virility, his lean sinewy body so near her own. Some of the harshness had gone out of his face since quoting the inscription, and a faint smile touched his lips. A great wave of love and longing rose in her, drowning her doubts. She loved him and he had offered her fulfilment. She would take a chance on him whatever the risks, if only he reciprocated her feeling in the smallest degree.

Impulsively she moved towards him, throwing her arms about his neck, clinging to him desperately, while she whispered:

'Love me, Mario, love me only a little, and nothing else matters.'

To her consternation, instead of reassuring her with tender words, his face turned white, and his mouth set in a grim line, while he tore her arms from around his neck, and thrust her violently away from him.

'For God's sake, Lorena, don't do that!' he said fiercely. Then as she gave him a stricken look, he added more gently: 'I have been most unwise. You must forgive me for making such a mistake.'

He walked away from her to the furthest corner of the terrace and proceeded to light another cigarette with trembling fingers.

The tide of Lorena's emotion receded. Feeling utterly repulsed, she stood staring blankly out over the sunlit garden. The only word which had registered in Mario's utterance was 'mistake'. So he had recognised the folly of their proposed marriage, no doubt with the assistance of Signor Segni. They had indeed been on the verge of making a terrible mistake, urged on by the intangible thing that was between them, the thing which in her had blossomed into love, but which for him was only the urgency of desire, and even that had inexplicably faded when she had sought his arms. Ironically it was the first time that she had sought their shelter, and her impulsiveness had earned her this repulse.

His voice, cold and incisive, cut through her chaotic thoughts.

'Are you ready to go now?'

'Yes, please,' she said dully. She saw that he was looking at her almost as if he disliked her and her heart sank even lower. What had gone wrong? Why, when she had reached the point of throwing all her doubts aside, had he so suddenly withdrawn? Even if he were belatedly regretting his insistence upon their engagement, could all feeling for her so quickly have fled?

'*Bene,*' he said brusquely. 'The car is outside.'

He moved swiftly through the house, leaving her to follow, as if he were trying to escape from her. The small discourtesy chilled her. He seemed as anxious to be rid of her as he had previously been eager to bring her to his house.

Mario required all his concentration to negotiate the steep descent into the town, while Lorena tried to assimilate this abrupt change from ardent lover, to remote stranger. It dated from the moment when he had returned with the ring and had been annoyed to find her with her hair loose. Had he then realised that she would never, as Margherita put it, make a suitable lady mayoress? Had he suddenly envisaged the tow-headed offspring? She sensed from the tenseness of his body that he was steeling himself against any further overture from her. He need not be afraid, she thought bitterly, she would never make another. Her spontaneous embrace had been an act of surrender a confession that she was prepared to accept every facet of his life if in return he would only assure her of a modicum of love. It was the first time that she had ever invited contact with him, and he had rejected her.

It seemed that he only wanted her when desire was pricking him, and that had already faded. She burned with shame as she realised that she had used his own tactics to weld him to her and they had lamentably failed.

But she could not accept his *volte-face* without protest and when they had reached the easier roads beyond the town, she would demand an explanation; insist that he was honest with her, and her mounting indignation did something to alleviate the terrible hurt of his rejection.

The opportunity was to be denied to her. Coming out of Nuoro, on a long stretch of road, they came upon a car pulled on to the verge with a flat tyre, and signalling to them to stop was a familiar figure in navy blue. Margherita Segni was a fast worker.

164

Mario brought the car slithering to a stop.

'*Dio*, Rita!' he exclaimed as he opened the door on his side, 'I only heard this afternoon that you had returned. I thought you were in Rome until August.'

He stepped down into the road beside her and she reached up and kissed his cheek.

'Couldn't keep away from you any longer, *caro mio*,' she said lightly. 'Aren't you glad to see me?'

'Delighted, of course, but you have stayed away too long,' he said sombrely, giving rise to a host of conjectures in Lorena's mind.

Had he been piqued by Margherita's prolonged absence and sought other diversions, finding them in herself, then discovering that she had returned, he had withdrawn from his later attachment? Margherita meant to recall him to his old allegiance, and it looked as if she was going to succeed, for he seemed to have forgotten Lorena's existence.

'Actually I had to return upon urgent business,' Margherita said, with a barbed glance towards Lorena. 'There are some things which are more important than having fun in Rome.'

'It has taken you quite a while to discover that,' Mario returned drily. He looked towards her car. 'Do you want help with changing the wheel?'

'I'm not going to attempt it,' Margherita told him decisively. 'I'm on my way to call on Viola and Pietro, I haven't seen them since they were married, and as you've come along so conveniently, perhaps you could give me a lift? I'll phone a garage from their place and ask them to collect the car. Pietro will run me back, I'm sure.'

Mario hesitated. 'It would not take me long,' he began.

'Not in that suit,' Margherita interrupted firmly. She looked at him admiringly. 'You're looking very smart and handsome as ever, *caro mio*. As regards my car, it isn't only the tyre, I think the steering needs a little attention. It hasn't been used while I was away.' Her eyes flickered to-

165

wards Lorena. 'Who's the girl-friend?' she asked in a perfectly audible aside.

Mario seemed to recollect Lorena's presence. He glanced at her, hesitated, then said: 'Lorena Lawrence ... Lorena,' he raised his voice, 'this is Margherita Segni.' He looked faintly embarrassed and Margherita smiled mischievously. 'She's staying with my grandmother,' he concluded.

'How nice for her,' Margherita observed. 'How do you do, Lorena?'

We've met before, the words hovered on Lorena's lips, but she checked them. She had not told Mario about her encounter with the Sardo girl, and to do so now would entail explanations which she did not want to give. Her heart was still hot and sore from Mario's rebuff, and he had not acknowledged her as his fiancée. She supposed that he could hardly do that without explanations on his part, which he would prefer to give to the Sardo girl in private. He had not expected her to return so soon, and had thought he would have plenty of time to acquaint her with the situation.

Margherita approached the open door of the car.

'I hope you're enjoying your visit to Sardinia, Lorena,' she enquired, her black eyes sparkling maliciously. 'You won't mind if Mario takes me as far as Pietro's place? It isn't far out of your way, if you're going back to the village.'

'Not in the least,' Lorena murmured mechanically, suspecting, and rightly, that the mishap to the car was a put-up job. Margherita knew they must return this way and had engineered the breakdown with the intention of intercepting them.

Margherita turned back to Mario. 'I shan't be intruding?'

'Of course not, Rita.' He opened the rear door for her, and she put her hand to her head.

'I wonder if Lorena would mind terribly if I sat in

front?' she asked. 'I've a bit of a headache, that burst tyre gave me a jolt, and there's more vibration in the back of a car...' She looked enquiringly from one to the other. 'Sorry to be so tiresome.'

Mario looked faintly surprised, while Lorena slipped out of the car, saying:

'I don't mind at all, *signorina.*'

'How nice of you,' Margherita said sweetly, 'but please call me Rita. I want all Mario's friends to be my friends.'

She took Lorena's place hurriedly, as if she feared Mario might object, but he accepted the exchange, almost, Lorena thought, with relief.

She settled herself in the back of the car, feeling that the situation had taken on the quality of a bad dream, a sad aftermath to the pleasant expedition of the morning.

'Bit of luck for me that you were passing,' Margherita announced cheerfully. She glanced back at Lorena. 'Been having a look round Nuoro?'

'It seems a nice place,' Lorena observed vaguely, wondering if Mario would confess where she had been, but he said nothing.

'Why don't you both come with me to Pietro's?' the girl rattled on. 'They're quite a nice young couple, you'd like them, Lorena, it would be a pleasant party.'

Before Lorena could reply, Mario said quickly:

'Lorena has had quite a day, I expect she is feeling too tired.'

'Can't she speak for herself?' Margherita asked slyly.

'Mario's right,' Lorena confirmed. 'I am too tired.'

She had had quite a day, she thought wryly, and she had no wish to visit Margherita's friends where she knew she would be made to feel an outsider. That was the object of the suggestion.

'Then you come, Mario,' Margherita said coaxingly. 'I'm sure you aren't tired. We can drop Lorena first and go on together, and then you can run me back.' As Mario looked

167

doubtful, she added persuasively, 'Pietro is one of your most enthusiastic supporters, he believes in all your ideas. You shouldn't neglect him.'

'I wonder how you know all that, seeing that you've spent the winter in Rome,' Mario commented drily. 'However, I've no objection to escorting you there, when we've dropped Lorena.'

Her point gained, Margherita continued to chatter gaily, mainly about their common acquaintances and their yachting adventures. Once she asked Lorena casually: 'Do you like sailing?' whereupon Mario replied for her:

'Lorena's experiences in that direction have been a little unfortunate.'

After that, Margherita ignored her completely. She edged closer to Mario until she touched his shoulder. He seemed to feel no constraint from her proximity; he appeared to be completely relaxed.

Her talk was freely interspersed with 'do you remembers', for she was emphasising for Lorena's benefit her long intimacy with the Marescus, and though Mario's response was at first a little taciturn, he soon thawed, and then they were both exchanging reminiscences with no thought for the still pale girl in the back seat. Occasionally Margherita would whisper something in Italian into Mario's ear, and more often than not he would laugh, apparently at some private joke.

Lorena stared at the two dark heads in front of her with a sick sensation. Mario seemed to have forgotten her presence altogether. Since she was to be disposed of before they went to their friends, she would have no chance to ask her questions, but they were no longer important. Mario was demonstrating very clearly that he regretted the necessity for marrying her and Margherita was proving her assertion that hers was the stronger tie. Possibly he was no longer in love with his childhood's sweetheart, but they had a whole history of joint memories and experiences behind them, and

168

his attitude towards her was much nearer to Lorena's concept of love than any fierce promptings of desire. A flash in the pan, Margherita had termed his infatuation for herself, and with her reappearance the flash had been extinguished. Moreover, Margherita was a Sard.

When they were alone, Mario would make his belated explanation of his reason for breaking his engagement, but Lorena was certain Margherita would have no difficulty in overcoming his scruples. The Sardo girl had shown herself to be infinitely resourceful.

Obviously Mario had not expected Margherita to return so soon and he had spoken with some asperity about her long absence. Possibly they had quarrelled about that one matter upon which they disagreed, but whatever that was, Margherita had come back determined to be reconciled, and he seemed to be sliding into his former intimacy with her very willingly. Lorena was now sure that there had been much more between them than he had admitted.

The long climb up to the village completed, Mario negotiated the twisty main street and drew up at Lucia's door. Lorena fumbled with the door handle, anxious to escape as quickly as possible, but the safety catch had caught and she could not open it. Mario sprang out of the car to come to her assistance, pausing a moment to brush something—was it Margherita's make-up?—from his shoulder, so that Margherita had time to lean over the back of her seat and whisper: 'First round to me, Rena.' Her black eyes were glittering with triumph.

Lorena descended from the car, ignoring Mario's outstretched hand. She could not bring herself to look at him, as she murmured:

'Goodbye, and thank you for everything.'

'*Ciao, carina*, I will be along tomorrow about midday,' he told her, but he spoke absently.

Margherita called, '*Addio!*' and waved her hand. Lorena responded with a mechanical ''Bye, Rita', and walked into the house.

From the shelter of the half opened door, she looked back. Mario had driven a short way further on and then pulled up. Both dark heads were bent over something, probably a route map. Then Margherita threw her arm across his shoulders, and he lifted his head. Lorena was not sure, but she thought that their lips met.

The car slid forward, but neither of them looked back.

Lorena had told Margherita that the choice between them lay with Mario and she had thought then that the odds were in her favour. That was before he had recoiled from her embrace. She had little doubt now that his talk with Signor Segni and the news of Margherita's return had brought home to him the folly of his involvement with herself. Margherita's father would have pointed out how well his daughter would fulfil the civic duties which would be expected of Mario's wife, and reminded him that he was officially bound to her. No doubt he too had heard rumours about a more recent attachment, and he would have made his point gracefully and tactfully. His words had had their effect upon Mario. He had shrunk from her upon his return to the house, because he had been made to realise that the price he must pay for her was too high. Then had come Margherita herself, reminding him of their past association, and displaying herself as a typical island girl, whose children would be as Sardo as she was.

Given a free choice, Lorena had little doubt which of them Mario would prefer.

She gave a long sigh and her gaze travelled to a gap between the houses opposite. Through it she could see the evening light lying over the rolling landscape in layers of gold, while purple haze gathered in the folds of the hills. She could have come to love this country if she had had to make it hers. There seemed to be no question of that now. She closed the door firmly upon Sardinia and her dreams and went into the sitting room.

Lucia rose from her chair as she appeared. 'Mario would not come in?' she asked.

'No, we picked up the Signorina Segni,' Lorena told her briefly. 'She had a puncture and he's taking her to her destination.'

'So she has come home,' Lucia said significantly. 'Perhaps she had heard ... rumours?'

Lorena said nothing, knowing this was true. She would have something to say to Venetia when next they met.

'I would like to speak to you,' Lucia went on. 'Come into the garden where we will not be disturbed. Assunta is putting Gigi to bed.'

From upstairs Assunta's soft voice floated down to them. She was crooning 'Santa Lucia.'

Lorena's already low spirits sank still lower. She was longing for the solitude and sanctuary of her own room, but she could not refuse Lucia's request without being rude. She followed her hostess into the walled garden, heavy with the scent of summer flowers. The surrounding walls were so high that nothing was visible except the bowl of the velvet sky in which the stars were beginning to appear. White moths were discernible in the dusk, tiny ghosts flickering over the blossoms.

Lucia sat down on a stone bench, impervious to its hardness, and wrapped her black shawl about her, but Lorena selected one of the more comfortable canvas chairs which Mario had brought up from Nuoro.

Lucia began abruptly: 'Mario was mad to bring you here, but I hoped it was only a temporary liaison and he would tire of you when he had had his way.'

'Oh, really, *signora*!' Lorena exclaimed, turning hot all over. 'I'm not that sort of girl.'

'So I'm told.' Lucia sounded sceptical. 'But I'm old-fashioned, I don't understand your foreign ways; *ecco*, it is not of those I want to speak. I've long been urging Mario to marry, but I never dreamed he would be so foolish as to

171

choose a foreigner, and he always swore he would only wed a Sard.'

'Please, *signora*,' Lorena said wearily, fearing a repetition of all the reasons why she should not marry Mario, 'you needn't say any more. I'm not going to marry your grandson.'

For that was the only possible solution, and she had come to accept it during the journey home while her two companions were demonstrating their pleasure in their reunion.

The light from the open back door illuminated Lucia's face, while Lorena's was in shadow. She saw the old woman's look of astonishment as she comprehended that the battle was over before she had even begun to fight. Surprise turned to doubt.

'You have quarrelled?'

'No ... well, actually I haven't told him yet.'

Lucia sighed. 'Then it is all ... what you say ... a storm in a teacup? He will not accept your decision and you will make it up.'

'No,' Lorena cried vehemently, 'we can't ... we mustn't, but he will accept it, I'm sure.'

'Did something happen in Nuoro this afternoon to upset you?' Lucia asked shrewdly.

Lorena told her about her encounter with Margherita.

'Who seems to have a prior claim,' she concluded drily.

Lucia chuckled with ironic amusement. 'She has not previously pressed it,' she remarked. 'But now she fears it is threatened, she changes her tune.' Her wrinkled face became solemn. 'She is the ideal wife for Mario,' she declared. 'If only he would take up with her again.'

'He's doing that,' Lorena said bitterly. 'But what about the gossip he was so anxious about? Could that really harm his career?'

'Not nearly as much as marrying you would,' Lucia said cruelly. 'But that can be circumvented. I shall suggest that he goes for a short vacation somewhere remote. When he

172

returns, he will give out that you changed your mind ... having made a better catch.' She chuckled again. 'There was one, wasn't there, among your fine friends?'

Giulio ... Lorena stared at her wondering if she did indeed have occult powers.

'How on earth did you know about that?' she breathed.

'Say a little bird told me, or my spirit guides,' Lucia suggested. 'So there was a rich suitor? *Bene*, then all the sympathy will be with Mario when it is discovered that you jilted him for greater wealth.'

'It seems I'm doomed to be thought a bitch,' Lorena sighed.

'In your country all the women are bitches, are they not?' Lucia announced sweepingly. She leaned forward trying to see the girl's face in the dark. 'When next he comes, I will tell Mario that, that you've gone back to your *amante* on the Costa Smeralda. I don't think he will think of you again after that.'

But Lorena protested, unwilling to blacken herself to such an extent. 'I ... I'll tell him myself,' she insisted. 'He's coming tomorrow, about midday.'

'You must be gone by then,' Lucia told her harshly. 'If you see him it will all begin again, for the further you retreat the more desirable you will become. That is the way of a man, for all that he'll deceive himself with the myth that it is necessary to protect your reputation.'

Lorena's blood stirred at Lucia's words. It was just possible that she was right. His masculine arrogance affronted by her decision to leave him, Mario's passion might flare up again—another flash in the pan? But if it did, it would be doused even more quickly than it had been that afternoon. However, it was much more likely that he would enlarge upon the mistake which they were making in the hope that she would release him, for that touchy honour of his might cause him to feel that he must keep his promise to her. Whatever attitude he took, their meeting was bound to be painful, and she was doubtful if she could relinquish him without showing her hurt. It would be much wiser to leave Lucia to deal with him, even though that meant she would present her motives in the worst possible light. But if she wanted to avoid him, she must leave and leave at once. She pointed this out to her companion, remarking that time was short.

'*Bene*, I will fix it,' the old woman assured her. 'The people at the post office are my friends. They will telephone for me if I insist that the matter is urgent. They will book a seat for you on a plane from Alghero in the morning. I will go and see them now.' She stood up. 'I am glad that you are being so sensible, Lorena,' she told her, using her first name, which caused Lorena to reflect that it was a cruel sequence of events which had made them allies. 'Believe me, you would not have been able to tolerate the life here. I realise this parting is painful for you, but it is nothing to the humiliations you would suffer if you stayed.'

She drew her shawl over her face until only her eyes were visible, a gesture from another age when women went veiled. Then she was gone, an ominous black shadow gliding through the dusk.

Lorena rose from her chair, feeling numb. It was done, the decisive step taken. She had better go and start packing, she supposed. She had severed her connection with Mario, but the full impact of her action had not yet struck her. Tomorrow, with luck, she would be back in Lincolnshire, pretending that nothing untoward had happened and no doubt her Sardinian visit would seem like a dream.

But in the solitude of her room, the storm broke over her. Despair, fierce jealousy, the anguish of loss. She sat down on her bed in the concealing darkness and wept bitterly.

She did not hear the sound of the door latch lifting, then Assunta was beside her, her arms about her, asking anxiously:

'Lorena, *cara*, what is it? You are all alone in the dark and crying.'

Desperately Lorena checked her sobs and felt for her handkerchief.

'It's nothing, Assunta,' she told her, gently disengaging herself from the girl's clinging arms. 'I'm overtired, so many excitements...' She began to laugh wildly.

'You hysterical,' Assunta said, and slapped her face.

Lorena became quiet.

'I will bring you a drink,' Assunta announced, 'and a light.'

Left alone Lorena fought to regain her self-possession. When Assunta returned with a lighted candle and a glass of lemonade, she had become calm, and she hoped the illumination was too weak to reveal her tear-stains.

'Thank you,' she said, taking the glass and sipping it gratefully. 'Sorry to make such a fool of myself. I *am* overtired, but I'm going away tomorrow, so you won't be bothered with me any longer.'

Assunta stood stock still. 'You were weeping for Mario?' she asked incredulously.

'Certainly not. One day with him has convinced me that he's quite impossible as a husband,' Lorena told her, speaking with forced gaiety. 'So it's all off. Your grandmother has thought of a way of averting the possibility of the scandal you were all so scared about, so it isn't necessary to get married after all, and I might as well go home. Incidentally, Margherita Segni has returned, and he's gone off with her now. With me out of the way he'll be able to marry his true Sard, and everyone will be happy ever after.' She stole a look at Assunta's face. She was looking completely unconvinced.

'I do not like Margherita,' she said stolidly. 'She does not love Mario, but she thinks he will be important man some day.'

'Well, if she doesn't, she put on a darned good act,'

175

Lorena's voice was brittle. 'And he was completely captivated.'

Assunta grimaced. 'So she up to her tricks again,' she remarked. 'But, Lorena, don't you love him?'

Lorena could not bring herself to make the denial, instead she endeavoured to say lightly:

'Love isn't everything, Assunta. He and I are not compatible.'

'Love is everything,' Assunta maintained stoutly. 'Love makes all things right.'

Omnia vincit amor—Lorena winced. 'So I thought once,' she agreed, 'but there has to be love on both sides, not merely a sense of honour,' unaware that she had completely betrayed herself to the watchful brown eyes.

'Mario come every day to comb your hair when you had fever,' Assunta remarked with seeming irrelevance. '*La nonna* was shocked and say she cut it off when he not there. I never see him more angry. He make her swear on the crucifix she not touch it.' Her eyes wandered to the dim outline of the cross upon the wall.

So he had told her himself, but she had suspected it was a pretty story concocted to please her, and now Assunta was verifying it. Lorena clenched her hands.

'But he wouldn't want to see my hair reproduced in his children,' she said bitterly.

'Who say that . . . *la nonna*?' Assunta asked sharply.

Lorena shook her head. It had been Margherita, but Lucia had probably had the same thought.

'I do not think it was Mario,' Assunta declared.

Lorena did not speak. Mario would not be such a cad as to mention it, but that did not mean it had not been in his mind when he had repelled her.

Lucia's voice came quavering up the stairs:

'Lorena . . . Assunta . . . it is all arranged!'

The two girls went to join her.

There had been no seats available on the flight from

Alghero next day, but there were vacancies on the afternoon flight from Cagliari to Rome, and one had been reserved for Lorena. Lucia had arranged with a nearby farmer, who was taking a load of cheeses into the capital early in the morning, to give Lorena a lift in his van.

'There is no time to hire a car from Nuoro,' she explained, 'and the journey will show you some more of the country.' She smiled a little maliciously. 'If there should be a search for you, it will naturally be made in Alghero.'

'Thank you,' Lorena said mechanically. It made little difference to her how or where she went since she had decided to go.

Assunta made neither protest nor comment upon the arrangements, but she continued to watch Lorena closely. Lorena smiled at her wanly, but she did not respond. Plainly she disapproved of the whole proceedings.

The van came round to fetch Lorena soon after dawn. It was a still grey day, and looked as if it might rain. The skies, she thought sadly, are the only things which will weep for my departure. But there she was wrong, for Gigi, who had insisted upon getting up to see her off, did shed tears over the loss of his comrade. Lorena comforted him with the promise of a small present to be sent to him as soon as she had arrived home. Lucia was impatient to see her safely off the premises, but of Assunta there was no sign.

'I wanted to say goodbye to her,' Lorena said anxiously, for she was fond of the girl, but she could not wait long, as the farmer was complaining that he should to be on his way.

Then Assunta came running down the street, carrying a tiny posy of wild flowers, thyme and small blossoms gathered on the mountain side. Her golden skin was glowing and her brown eyes shining with secret triumph, so that Lucia looked at her suspiciously.

But all she said was, 'For you, it will pin on your jacket,

a memento of the countryside,' and thrust the nosegay into Lorena's hands.

The tears rose to Lorena's eyes, as she thanked her. The little flowers had been blooming all round the hut on that memorable morning, when she and Mario had eaten their breakfast of trout and goat's milk. Lucia said scornfully something about wasting time over sentimental trifles, while Lorena kissed Gigi and Assunta, then climbed into the van beside the driver. She had left no message for Mario when he came, Lucia had declared it was better not to do so, and she would deal with him. Lorena knew what she would tell him, that she had gone back to her old life, unable to face the prospect of giving it up, and perhaps to Giulio. Though the thought of his contempt was hurtful, it meant the break between them could never be healed and he could go to his Margherita with a clear conscience.

Her driver could speak only a few words that were comprehensible to her, and in any case the rattling of his ramshackle old van made conversation difficult. Lorena was not sorry, for she was soon lost in memories. Their way led along the edge of the Gennargentu, where the peaks were dark and clear against the pewter sky. She was reminded at every twist and turn of the day when Mario had brought her up there. How angry she had been with him, though even then, she had been fighting the spell of his magnetic personality. Ice and fire, and the ice had melted, only to be frozen again to perpetual frigidity, for no other man would ever move her as he had done and the future had a glacial aspect.

Such a short time had elapsed, the mere passing of May into June, but her springtime was over, her love had flowered and faded. From henceforth she would be poised, mature and untouchable, and the desolate feeling of irreparable loss which was engulfing her, would in time fade away, to be succeeded by self-congratulation that her wisdom and foresight had led her to escape from an impossible situation.

The road descended from the mountain fringe to rolling country. Hay, corn and stretches of pyrethrums in bloom replaced the oaks and scrub. Low hills, either bare or covered with short turf, superseded the wooded heights. These in turn gave place to a big plain, intensively cultivated, mostly occupied with vineyards and orchards.

The van rattled along at a surprisingly good pace, and there was little traffic at that early hour. They did encounter several farm carts drawn by oxen, occupying the middle of the road, the slow motions of which to get out of the way called for maledictions upon their heads from the van driver.

Cagliari, the capital of the island, was a city which epitomised the confused and bitter history of the country. Occupied by Romans, Pisans and Spaniards, their various influences were identifiable in the old quarter of the town, from the remains of a Roman amphitheatre its seats carved out of living rock to the surviving Pisan towers, with here and there a Catalan archway.

The modern city was spread along the waterfront. The Poetta beach at its eastern extremity was a stretch of white sand beside a shallow sea, with all the sophisticated trimmings of an up-to-date playground, including restaurants and cafés.

The van driver dumped Lorena in the centre of the town, and refused her offer of recompense with a proud gesture.

'For the Signora Marescu I will do anything,' he told her in halting Italian. 'She save the life of my child.'

So Lucia's witch doctoring paid dividends. Probably the post office family in the village were equally beholden to her.

Having made such an early start, there was a lot of time to fill before Lorena was due at the airport. A helpful policeman told her where she could hire a car, and she asked the driver to show her something of the town before

179

he drove her thither. He was a lively little Italian and he took her under his wing. The Poetta Beach, he decided, was where most people wished to go, and drove his passenger along the waterfront in its direction.

When they arrived there, he was disappointed to find only a few people were about, and only a few intrepid swimmers in the water. Sea and sand looked desolate under a grey sky. He blamed the early morning hour, for it was in the evening that the beaches came to life. He described how the young of both sexes disported themselves after work, the bikini-clad girls, gold of skin, their hair blowing in the breeze, wandered up and down in groups, kicking the sand and pretending to ignore the lithe bronzed young men, alternately swimming, playing football or, in their turn, merely strolling. It was, he declared, the Poetta version of the village *corso*, the nightly promenade of youth with its speculative assessment of the charms of the opposite sexes. The *signorina* had seen a *corso*, of course, where the young men looked with the eyes of the wolf, and the girls pretended to be lambs? Lorena said that she had in various Latin small towns.

As if trying to atone for the drabness of the weather, he told her she should stay until sunset; the sunsets at Cagliari were the finest in the whole island, the sun going down in a blaze of colour to be succeeded by a mauve and indigo dusk, and though that morning there was no sun, a luminosity in the zenith suggested it might appear later on.

Lorena said she was sure the spectacle was marvellous but she must be on her way long before sundown.

The little man seemed distressed that such a beautiful young lady should be all alone, but perhaps some *amante* awaited her coming on the mainland?

For his benefit, Lorena invented a tale about a visit to a relative, and an ardent lover impatiently awaiting her return, but no one would watch for her arrival in Rome and she was leaving her heart behind her. It was nearly midday,

180

and by now Mario would have gone to the village, and Lucia would have told him of her flight, and done her best to derogate her. He would revert to his original opinion of her, and any faint regret he might feel would soon be dissolved by Margherita.

She asked her chauffeur to find for her a quiet place for lunch and invited him to share it with her, but that he declared was too great an honour, but sensing she was feeling lonely, he suggested taking her to his brother who had a small *ristorante* on the seafront, where she would receive a warm welcome.

It turned out to be a homely little place, where, as promised, the proprietor and his wife beamed at her, and since it was early, and there were no other customers she had their undivided attention. The meal was simple and well cooked, freshly grilled sardines, pasta and the familiar ewes' milk cheese, though it might have been dust and ashes as far as Lorena was concerned. However, she did make an effort to respond to the friendliness of her hosts, and this was helped by the intervention of their numerous offspring, brown, black-eyes creatures, who kept creeping in from the kitchen to stare curiously at the fair-haired *signorina*, until they were shooed back by their rubicund father.

'Scusi—scusi,' he said each time after they had been removed. 'They think that you are an angel come to visit us. *Mio bambino*, the smallest one, say you like the picture above his bed, but that you have no wings.'

Lorena was grateful to them all for diverting her sad thoughts, and she left to a chorus of '*presto ritorno*', but she would never come to Sardinia again.

Her driver, who had been accommodated with lunch in the kitchen, proceeded to enlarge upon the family prospects, past, present and to come, but she scarcely heard him. She was bidding Mario and his country a last farewell.

She arrived at the airport in plenty of time to pick up her reservation, and bade the little man an almost affectionate

181

goodbye. Had he but known it he had helped her through her darkest hour.

She sat in the lounge waiting for her flight to be called, idly watching the milling crowd of passengers, mainly tourists and Italians. Airports are much the same throughout the world, and in spirit she had already left the island.

Resolutely she turned her mind away from the past and concentrated upon the future.

From Rome she would be able to get a plane to England, and it would be nice to see her parents again and tell them about ... the fashion show, which seemed half a century ago. If she had to wait for a reservation, she would look up Venetia. Although she was angry with her for chattering out of turn, it did not matter now, and her astringent views upon love and marriage would have a tonic effect.

After a brief stay at home, she would look up her agent. She had missed several tentative engagements by her prolonged absence, but she remembered that there had been a suggested trip to Canada to photograph furs against their natural background. She hoped it was still on. The Canadian scene would be vastly different from the Mediterranean, and out there it would be easier to forget.

Her flight was indicated, and she went out on to the tarmac, and the waiting plane. She climbed up the steps, trying not to recall her journey to the island in Signor Ricci's jet, when she had first met Mario. So after all she was going back to the modelling which he so disliked, making a spectacle of herself, he had said, but she would be well covered in the fur coats and stoles she would be displaying in Canada, she thought wryly.

She shared a double seat with a middle-aged Italian, who courteously insisted that she should sit next the window. The steps were being withdrawn, when there was a brief altercation outside and a last-minute passenger was hustled on to the plane. The machine began to taxi towards the runway and Lorena watched out of the window the last of the island going by.

The morning's gloom had passed and the sun had come out, as the plane climbed up into an azure sky. For a little while after take-off, Lorena saw the island spread beneath her, its mountain crests and wide valleys, its white towns and grey villages. Then the aircraft gained altitude and swept out over the sea. Passengers released their seat belts and the smokers lit their cigarettes as the lighted notice forbidding them went out.

Someone came down the aisle and touched the Italian on the shoulder, with a whispered request. In response to it, he rose from his seat.

'*Si, si, signor*, with pleasure.'

He went out into the aisle to find the seat the other man had vacated, who in his turn sat down beside Lorena.

'*Buon giorno, signorina*,' Mario said.

CHAPTER NINE

LORENA had been wrapped in reverie during the exchange between the two men, and Mario's familiar voice seemed part of her dream, until she turned slowly in her seat and found he was in reality beside her. Caught off guard, her eyes and mouth betrayed her, so much so that he said, with a twitch of his lips:

'I believe you are pleased to see me.'

Hastily she looked away, while she told him in a carefully controlled voice:

'I'm overwhelmed by surprise.'

How had he discovered that she was flying from Cagliari? No one knew except Lucia and Assunta. The latter might have communicated with him, though she could not imagine how, and certainly Lucia would not have mentioned her destination, since she was so anxious to part them. But speculation was quickly swamped by other sensations. Her unruly heart was beating a tattoo of glad recognition, while her brain registered confused amazement.

With deliberation, Mario put a hand under her chin, and turned her face towards him, but she kept her lids lowered against his questing gaze.

'Why are you running away from me?' he asked. 'What have I done?'

That roused her.

'What haven't you done?' she returned reproachfully, pushing his hand away. 'What about Margherita? I'm not quite blind, you know.'

'Jealous?' he asked with satisfaction.

'Not at all, but as I seem to be quite superfluous, I'm going back to my old job.'

'That you are not,' he informed her, feeling for the inevi-

184

table cigarettes.

'You smoke too much,' she told him severely.

'Only since I met you. I find I frequently need to steady my nerves.'

'So I'm to blame for that too?' she said tartly. 'Really, you can't hold me responsible for all your bad habits, as well as your misadventures.'

'But you were the root of all of them,' he told her reproachfully. 'You have caused complete havoc in my life, and have forced me to forswear myself upon more than one count. Now you are trying to run out on me. That is not fair, *carissima*.'

'Isn't it?' She tried to meet his gaze, but the familiar smouldering fire in the depths of his eyes caused her to look away. 'You need no longer be forsworn with Margherita,' she went on in a cool voice. 'I've abdicated.'

He busied himself lighting his cigarette, then he told her.

'It may interest you to know that I had a flaming row with her after we left you yesterday and we did not go to see her friends. I drove her straight back to her car, which was perfectly okay. She had only let the air out of the tyre.'

'I'm not surprised to hear that, but I'm not available to console you because you've fallen out with your fiancée,' Lorena retorted. She was bewildered and puzzled by his unexpected appearance, but she was not going to allow herself to be whistled back like an obedient dog for the purpose of annoying Margherita. They could make up their quarrel without using her as a stooge.

'I thought you were that,' he said calmly, drawing on his cigarette. 'Margherita never was. It is true that my grandmother and her father tried to arrange an engagement between us, and she did seem a possibility since I had to have a wife, but she told me she would only marry me if I would give up my work and live with her in Rome, in short, become her lapdog. That of course I refused to do.'

The one point of difference which Margherita had been confident that she could overcome.

'That was several years ago,' Mario went on. 'She has not changed, but I have.'

'You mean you're now prepared to accept her terms?' Lorena asked doubtfully.

'Would I, hell!' he returned forcibly. 'No, Lorena, I said I had changed. Don't you want to know in what way?'

'It's nothing to do with me,' she said frigidly. 'How did you know I'd be on this plane?'

'It has everything to do with you, and the plane was due to Assunta, bless her. She sent me a note this morning by a man who comes to work in Nuoro. Unfortunately he was not very expeditious about delivering it. I only just made it.'

Assunta with the glowing cheeks and secret triumph in her eyes. So that was what she had been doing so early in the morning, and the bunch of flowers was only camouflage to conceal her errand from Lucia's suspicious eyes. Assunta believed that Lorena loved Mario, and had put him on her track, but she was not grateful to her for her intervention. It only meant that she would have to break with Mario all over again.

'I'm afraid you've had a journey for nothing,' she said desperately. 'It's no use, Mario, I can't marry you. We're too far apart.'

'Don't you think we could bridge the gap if we put our hearts into it?'

'That's just it, your heart isn't in it. You don't love me.'

'What makes you think that?'

She raised startled grey eyes to meet his intent dark ones.

'The way you repulsed me at your house,' she whispered.

'God in heaven!' he exploded, and several other passengers looked round with interest. He lowered his voice to continue. 'Lorena, you little cretin, didn't you understand? I feared to let myself go. That long day together was a

186

mistake, with you in my house, like my wife, but not my wife. I did not realise when I asked you to come what a strain it would be, and you did not help. I am not a saint, *cara*, and St. Antony himself would have fallen for you that day. The intimacy of the bathroom, the way you looked when I returned with your hair loose and innocent allure in every line of you.' He took out his handkerchief and wiped his forehead at the recollection. 'Love me a little, you said, when I was yearning for you with every fibre of my being, and your arms were an invitation I had to fight to resist.'

'I ... I didn't think,' Lorena faltered, overcome by this confession of masculine fallibility. 'I'd no idea I was such a Circe. But, seriously, is that enough? Your grandmother told me that you have a great political future and marriage with a Sard would assist your career, while I would only be an encumbrance.'

'My grandmother is an interfering old woman,' he said tersely. 'But of course the failure of my father's marriage shook her. It does not follow that ours would fail, and you would charm all my supporters as you have enslaved me. You must not underrate yourself; you have poise and chic, you would do any man credit, and I shall be proud to own you as my wife.'

This assessment was reassuring, but it still did not make her a Sard. Nothing could do that. Mario looked at her troubled face, and enquired:

'You like my country, don't you? You would not find it impossible to live there?'

Impulsively she turned to him. 'I could live in much worse places with you,' she admitted, her resistance ebbing.

Her anxious eyes searched his face, wondering if she dare mention the tow-haired brood, but Mario was curiously reticent about some subjects, and she dared not broach the possibility. After all, it was only a possibility.

'There is one thing I should confess to you,' he continued, and her heart leaped painfully. Was it coming now,

187

since he was looking embarrassed? 'My share of my father's patrimony was land in Gallura, and that is paying dividends with the new developments there. I ploughed the money back into hotels and all the other amenities. ... What is it?' for her eyes had widened in indignation.

'You hypocrite!' she exclaimed. 'After all your criticism of the consortium, you now admit that you belong to it. You joined with the others to corrupt the poor, proud Sards.' She began to laugh. 'Oh, Mario, you'll tell me next you advocate the *dolce vita*!'

'That I do not,' he retorted. 'The change, *cara mia*, is inevitable, and since I can do nothing to stem it, I console myself by trying to preserve what little I can of the spirit of old Sardinia. I work hard for her welfare, and I would not dream of spending my wealth on mere self-gratification. After all, the change is bringing in work and prosperity, as you pointed out yourself with some heat.'

'This is where we came in,' Lorena observed. 'What happens now?'

'Where are you making for?'

'England and home. My parents will be thinking I've got lost.'

'So be it,' he said. 'It is time I met them, and perhaps your father can give me some instruction in modern farming.'

She stared at him wide-eyed. 'You ... you're coming with me?' she gasped.

'Of course. I am not going to let you out of my sight again. We will get married as soon as possible. Perhaps we can wheedle a special licence out of your Archbishop, but our honeymoon we will spend on Capri. At least the sunshine there is more or less guaranteed, while it always rains in your country.'

'Not always.' She looked at him with dancing eyes. 'I never can resist you,' she sighed. 'So I suppose I'll have to agree.'

'If only we were not on this goddam aeroplane, I would make you more enthusiastic than that,' he complained.

'Perhaps it's safer,' she suggested demurely.

'Definitely, but you wait until we are married, my little gilt-haired witch. I will get my own back then.'

'I'm sure you will,' she murmured, while the hot colour flooded her cheeks.

He took her hand in his and said with a tenderness of which she had not believed he was capable:

'You need not fear me, Lorena, I will do nothing to abuse your love. Assunta in her note said you were crying last night because of me. I hope I may never cause you to weep again.'

Regardless of onlookers, she impulsively raised his hand and laid it against her face.

'If you do, darling, they will be tears of joy,' she told him tremulously.

The purple pall of a night spangled with patterns of stars hung over the crags and ribbons of light which were Capri, while the sea washed against its rocks in a murmuring lullaby.

Lorena sat before her dressing table in nylon negligée, brushing the silky strands of her hair.

It was all over, the time of waiting, during which Mario had got on extraordinarily well with her father, and her mother though a little in awe of him had said he was the most fascinating man she had ever met, the quiet wedding —neither had wanted a big affair—and now at last they were alone together.

Soft-footed, a dark figure came from the bathroom, arrayed in a heavy silk robe, and brown sinewy fingers took the brush from her hand. With light, deft strokes, Mario continued the operation until her hair sprayed out like golden foam, clinging to his sleeve.

Dropping the brush, he sank on his knees beside her,

encircling her waist with his arms, and burying his face against her breast.

'It was your hair I loved first, *carissima*,' he murmured. 'If we have a child, I hope it will be blessed with it.'

Thus was Lorena's last doubt dissipated. She bent her head to meet his lips, while her hair covered them both like a shining cloak.

Have You Missed Any of These Harlequin Romances?

All books are 60c. Please use the handy order coupon.

K